FAKE NEWS:
Strange historical facts
reimagined in the world of
Donald Trump

By
David Hutter

About this book

With fictional Donald Trump anecdotes that are based on the mess created by some of history's greatest megalomaniacs and worst decision-makers, this satire offers the small consolation that while things are bad right now, the world has been here before...

Focusing on the Donald's attitude towards North Korea and his sycophantic advisers, as well as the 'special relationship' between the US and the UK, this novella draws on bizarre and obscure historical facts from, for instance, ancient China, Tudor England, revolutionary France and the Cold War. Those facts — which include a rabbit attack, the accidental loss of nuclear bombs and the ceremonial burial of presidential body parts — are described at the end of each chapter.

Disclaimer

There is no suggestion that the fictional elements of this book – that is, anything other than the "What really happened" sections – are based on the actual behaviour of the persons mentioned therein.

Contents

CHAPTER ONE
Wires crossed

It was 4.15am on the January morning after his inauguration day, and the new President of the United States, Donald Trump, was standing by the Georgian windows in the Oval Office, plotting to become the most famous POTUS ever. Looking out into the darkness beyond the frost-covered South Lawn, he spotted the lit-up Washington Monument in the distance. The obelisk reminded him of the nearby Lincoln Memorial, the perversely magnificent marble tribute to someone who, by abolishing slavery, had caused so much grief to the white people that defined America. And suddenly, he had an idea.

Sitting down at his desk, he switched on his computer and rang White House Press Secretary Sean Spicer, who sleepily answered the phone at his home in a leafy, suburban part of nearby Alexandria, Virginia.

"Spicer," he said, while logging on to Twitter, "we're replacing the statue at the Lincoln Memorial with one of me and renaming the whole thing the Trump Memorial. I'm about to announce it on Twitter, but I need you to tell the media, as well."

Instantly wide awake, Spicer said: "Mr President, I don't think that's a good idea, especially not on your first day in office."

"But I'm the best President ever!"

"Yes, but we need more evidence to back it up."

"I've got a letter from my doctor saying I'm the healthiest President ever and that my test results were astonishingly excellent."

"I don't think the media will consider that a reason to replace Lincoln's statue."

"I hate the media," Trump grumbled. "They treat me very, very unfairly. So, let's just announce it on Twitter and leave it at that."

"Please don't do that," Spicer begged. "Let's discuss it with the rest of your team first."

Sighing, Trump said: "OK, let's have an emergency meeting in twenty minutes."

At 4.45am on this wintry Saturday, Spicer therefore rushed into the by now chaotically buzzing Oval Office, where general confusion about the purpose of this meeting in the middle of the night was complemented by a sense of panic. This was writ large on the faces of White House Chief of Staff Reince Priebus, Secretary of the Treasury Steve Mnuchin, Counselor to the President Kellyanne Conway, Trump's daughter Ivanka and her husband Jared Kushner, with only White House Chief Strategist

Steve Bannon grinning because the new administration was already disrupting the stale complacency of the venerable halls.

"There you are," Trump said, as the Press Secretary entered. "Folks, the reason why I have called this meeting is that Sean and I have decided to replace the statue at the Lincoln Memorial with one of me and to rename the whole thing the Trump Memorial."

Bannon, the former Executive Chair of the President-endorsed conspiracy website Breitbart, nodded approvingly. But everyone else looked shocked and turned to Spicer, who anxiously shook his head and mouthed: "Not me! Not me!"

"And to honour the movement Breitbart started," Trump continued, "and based on which we'll shake up American politics, I will rename this place the Alt-White House."

"That's a great idea," Bannon said, "except the movement is called the alt-right, not the alt-white."

"Are you sure about that?" he asked, eyeing him suspiciously.

"He's right, Dad," Ivanka said quickly.

Surprised, Trump looked at her. Then he turned to Bannon again and said: "OK, I trust Ivanka."

"I trust her, too," Mnuchin said, and received a quizzical look from Conway.

"Thanks, Mnuchin, you're a great guy – the best," Trump replied, and Conway's look of surprise turned into a scowl. "Let's stick with the name White House, then, especially considering that we're white supremacists."

"Please don't say that publicly," Spicer pleaded. "CNN and *The New York Times* will kill you otherwise."

Banging his fist on his desk, Trump said: "I've had enough of political correctness – I will tell it like it is! The fake media is the enemy of the American people, and they treat me very, very unfairly. And by the way, I almost fought in Vietnam in the sixties, so I know what can really kill you – and believe me, it's not CNN or *The New York Times*."

"Please don't mention the Vietnam War either," the Press Secretary implored him. "The media went nuts when you told them you'd got lucky in the draft lottery given that everyone knows you received a medical exemption because of your feet."

"My draft number was phenomenal!" Trump exclaimed. "And I don't have any medical problems – my doctor said my physical strength and stamina are extraordinary!"

"Yes, but he said that a few months ago, not in 1969."

"He's right, Dad," Ivanka said, while the President glared at Spicer. "You did get a medical exemption because you had bone spurs in your heels – you've showed me the letter a few times." Then she went over to his side of the desk, touched his shoulder and softly added: "Let's just forget about the statue for now and go back to sleep. We don't want to make any rash decisions on our first day at the White House."

As her father reluctantly grumbled his assent, everyone breathed a sigh of relief. "OK, leave now," he said, waving his hand dismissively as he restarted his computer.

Exiting the Oval Office, Spicer turned around when he reached the door and said: "Please don't tweet anything before running it by me first."

"Shut the door!" Trump snapped, without looking up from his screen. Then he logged on to Twitter, and his index fingers furiously crashing down on the keyboard, he wrote: "I just had an emergency meeting with Secretary of Defense Jim Mattis and the best military advisers in the world, and we've decided to launch a surprise nuclear strike against North Korea at 3am on Monday!"

Pleased to finally have left his mark as President, he then got down to the day-to-day business of running the country, tweeting "Meryl Streep is the most over-rated actress in Hollywood!!!" and "Robert Pattinson should not take back Kristen Stewart – she cheated on him like a dog and will do it again!"

Moments later, all hell broke loose as everyone rushed back into the Oval Office.

"Dad, you can't start a nuclear war!" Ivanka called out.

"Why not?"

"Because it's insane!"

Frowning at her, he said: "My two greatest assets are mental stability and being, like, really, really smart, so you can't say it's insane because you have no evidence for it."

"What you're saying is fake news!" Conway snapped at Ivanka.

In response, the President glowered at Conway, and Mnuchin said: "No, it's not. It would be fake news if you had said it, but you can't accuse Ivanka of spreading fake news – that would be very, very unfair."

"Thanks, Mnuchin, you're a great guy – the best," Trump said, as the phone on his desk started ringing. Picking up the receiver, he heard a lady nervously say: "Hello Mr President, it's Theresa May."

"Theresa who?" he asked, while making shushing noises to the people in the room.

"Theresa May," she repeated.

"Is this about an alimony lawsuit? If it is, you have to call my lawyers."

"No, I'm Britain's Prime Minister," she said, before he could hang up.

Speaking into the mouthpiece, he asked his entourage: "Is Britain's Prime Minister a woman?"

"Yes, she's called Theresa May," Kushner said.

"Is she hot?"

Taken aback, his son-in-law hesitated, but Bannon and Mnuchin shook their heads.

"Maggie, it was very nice to talk to you, but I have to hang up now," Trump said.

"I just wanted to tell you," she said quickly, "that I just found out about your plans for North Korea, and I wanted to let you know that the UK fully supports you as a sign of the special relationship that exists between our countries."

"OK, bye now," he said, and hung up.

Instantly, everybody in the Oval Office started talking at Trump. But then his phone rang once more and he picked up the receiver.

"Sir, this is Jim Mattis. I just read your message regarding our meeting about North Korea."

"And?"

"That meeting never took place!" the Secretary of Defense exclaimed. "Plus, starting a nuclear war is insane!"

"That's fake news – someone just told me that."

"Who?"

Wrong-footed, Trump scanned the faces in the room. "A very, very special person who I've met many, many times. He or she is very trustworthy."

"Just a moment," Mattis said, "I'll add General Dunford and General Milley to the line – I've asked them to dial in."

"I've got work to do now," Trump replied, and hung up, while everyone in the room started talking again.

"Sir, you can't launch a nuclear war now because we must get rid of immigrants in the US first before we start getting rid of them in their own countries," Bannon said.

"Plus, the media will go nuts!" Spicer said.

"And remember that war is expensive," Kushner cautioned.

"Dad, you really cannot do this!" Ivanka insisted.

Banging his fist on the desk, he said: "I am the President of the United States, so I can do whatever I want to do!" Pointing at the door, he added: "And now I want you out – all of you!"

While everyone shuffled off, he said: "Except Mnuchin."

As the Treasury Secretary's face lit up, Kellyanne Conway gave him a jealous look. "Shut the door behind you," he gleefully said to her.

Meanwhile, Trump indicated for him to take a seat on the other side of his desk and said: "Mnuchin, I want you to be completely honest with me – do you think we're moving too fast with this war? I need your opinion because I trust you."

"I don't think we're moving too fast," he replied. "If we want to make America great again, we have to start as soon as possible."

"That's what I think. But Jared said war is expensive."

"Sir, if I'm honest, I wouldn't trust him or any of the other people who were here just now, except for Ivanka. Apart from her, everyone has their own agenda."

"You think so?" Trump asked, worried.

"Yes, Sir. Because if you think about it, the war won't cost us anything at all – you'll simply make the North Koreans pay for it after we've nuked them."

"But do they have any money?" Trump asked warily. "Because that's why we're fighting them, right? Because they're poor."

"I'm not entirely sure about the ins and outs of this war."

Confused, Trump said: "I thought that was the reason. Anyway, I've got a better idea." Then he turned to his computer and added: "I've got work to do now."

As Mnuchin left the Oval Office, Kellyanne Conway was waiting for him in the hallway of the West Wing and immediately pounced.

"You are trying to be his little munchkin, aren't you?"

"No, not at all," he said defensively. "I just like his policies."

"What policies?" she asked, and scrutinised his face.

"Well, he wants to make America great again."

"That's not a policy – it's bullshit, and you know it," she said. Moving her face closer to his, she hissed: "Just be careful, munchkin – I've got my eyes on you!"

Then she stormed off just as White House Chief of Staff Reince Priebus brushed past them and knocked on the door to the Oval Office. After the President had asked him to enter, he closed the door again and said: "Sir, I just received word that the President of South Korea, Kim Jung-Pyo, and Britain's Prime Minister Theresa May are on their way to Washington."

Staring at his computer screen, Trump said: "I'm looking at pictures of that woman. Bannon was sugarcoating it when he said she isn't hot – she's incredibly old, almost my age."

"She'll be arriving at the White House at approximately four o'clock this afternoon, while Mr Kim is scheduled to arrive at around ten o'clock this evening."

"Why are they coming here now?" he asked, frowning at the Chief of Staff. "My inauguration was yesterday. Mind you, there were so many people there, they wouldn't have got a seat."

"I understand they're coming here to discuss your nuclear strike."

"There's nothing to discuss," Trump replied impatiently. "It's a surprise."

"I understand the Korean President is worried about the potential impact nuclear war might have on his country."

"Why? Does he think there's just one Korea?" Trump sneered. "We're attacking only the northern one, not the other three."

"It may have been lost in translation – if his aides are anything to go by, Kim's English isn't great."

"And why is the old English woman coming here?"

"I'm not sure," Priebus replied.

"I'll make them wait until midday tomorrow," the President said testily. "They can't just turn up here uninvited and expect me to be free when it suits them."

At about quarter past three that afternoon, shortly after they'd landed at Reagan National Airport in Arlington, Virginia, May and her entourage exited the plane via the jetway and walked towards the arrivals hall, where dozens of journalists were already waiting, eager to hear why she'd travelled to the United States.

Getting off his phone as they approached a moving walkway, one of her aides said: "Prime Minister, I've just been told by a member of Mr Trump's team that the President won't see you until midday tomorrow."

Shell-shocked, she stopped in her tracks. "What do you mean, he won't see me until midday tomorrow?"

"He won't see you until midday tomorrow."

"He can't do that – I'm Britain's Prime Minister, for Christ's sake! I've flown all the way to Washington to see him. It would be utterly humiliating if he doesn't see me now, especially in the context of today's riots."

Standing around awkwardly, May's aides stared at their feet and didn't say anything.

"Say something!" she snapped. "What should I do now?"

"You have to spin it in a way to make it sound like it was your idea to delay the meeting," one of her staff members replied.

"How could I possibly explain that I came here on the day of the riots although I didn't want to meet him today?" she hissed.

"Just say you asked him for more time to prepare because North Korea is a complex issue."

Sighing, May straightened her jacket. "OK, let's go, then."

Five minutes later, she nervously smiled at the reporters in the arrivals hall and coughed repeatedly to get them onside before explaining the purpose of her visit.

"At this crucial time for our closest ally, as the United States are preparing to go to war to preserve our Western democratic values, it is of utmost importance to the United Kingdom to stand side by side with our friends and reinforce the special relationship that exists between our countries," she said.

"Does Mr Trump even know you're here?" a reporter asked.

"Of course, he does," she said acidly. "I would not have travelled all the way to Washington without having been invited."

"So, he wanted you to come here?" another journalist asked.

"My private conversations with the President are confidential."

"But why did you fly out today considering that your meeting is tomorrow and that there were violent protests against your welfare cuts in Britain today? Shouldn't you be back home right now?"

"I am obviously deeply saddened by the terrible events that took place in London and other parts of the UK today. But as Britain's Prime Minister, it is my responsibility and my great privilege to support the United States in testing times such as these because of the shared history between our nations and the special relationship we have as a result. Given the complexities surrounding North Korea, I agreed with Mr Trump to meet tomorrow rather than today to give me more time to prepare for our talks. And that's what I will do now. Thank you very much."

Then she staggered off in her high heels to a waiting car, and to prevent the President from interrupting her preparations for their vital meeting, she decided against staying at the White House and instead retreated to the privacy of a hotel near the airport.

The following morning at 4.30am, Donald Trump kick-started an anything but peaceful Sunday by furiously typing on his computer in the Oval Office. "As of last night," he wrote on Twitter, "the United States are deploying troops and fighter jets armed with nuclear bombs to South Korea for our invasion of North Korea. And believe me: we'll win bigly!!!"

Two hours later, Secretary of Defense Jim Mattis called to clarify that the troops and aircraft carriers he'd mentioned over dinner the previous evening had, in fact, been stationed in South Korea since 1953.

"Why did you feed me fake news, Mattis?" Trump hissed into the receiver. "Are you a South Korean spy?"

"The South Koreans are our allies."

"This is your final warning, Mattis – next time, you're fired!"

Then the President hung up and furiously took to Twitter again to further up the ante, promising, "In the next 24 hours, there'll be doom and gloom for North Korea!!!", before adding cryptically, "South, East and West!"

As news outlets around the world anxiously tried to figure out what the postscript meant, he received his first foreign visitors at the Oval Office at midday. While White House Chief of Staff

Reince Priebus ushered in the British Prime Minister and a slim, about fifty-year-old Asian man in a black suit, the US Commander in Chief remained seated behind his desk. Stony-faced and pretending to be signing important documents, he looked up only momentarily and sternly said: "Maggie, close the door."

Closing it while her host focused on practising his signature, May chuckled nervously and said: "It's Theresa, by the way."

"Huh?" he replied, and looked at her. Then he put his pen down, pointed at the chairs on the other side of his desk and coolly said to both of them: "Take a seat."

As soon as they'd sat down, he extended his right arm slightly, so that they had to get up to shake his hand. "I'm Donald Trump," he said, while Priebus came over to stand behind him. "President of the United States of America."

"I'm Kim Jung-Pyo, President of South Korea," his counterpart said frostily, and shook hands with Trump, who twisted his arm, though just about soft enough to keep him from complaining.

Sitting down again, Kim rubbed his hurting right shoulder with his left hand and glowered at his host. Meanwhile, the latter patted May's hand before addressing both of them as he asked: "Why are you here?"

"Because of your nuclear war!" Kim snapped, incensed by the question.

"But it hasn't started yet."

"We don't even know if you're going to attack at 3am in Washington or 3am in Korea, which is in two hours!" Kim exclaimed.

"We don't know either," he calmly replied. "As I said, it's a surprise attack. I learnt that tactic when I almost fought in Vietnam in the sixties. And by the way, in the end, I got a deferral because I had smelly feet."

"Bad feet," Priebus said.

"Bullshit," Trump hissed. "Sometimes, my feet are a bit smelly when I take off my shoes, but that's it." Smiling at his guests, he added: "In any case, having unprotected sex in the eighties without contracting HIV is my personal Vietnam – it makes me feel like a great and very brave soldier."

"And the UK stands firmly behind you if you're going to war again now, Mr President," May said eagerly. Since he didn't react, she added: "That's because of the special relationship between our countries."

Turning to Kim, Trump asked: "Do we have a special relationship with your country, too?"

"No," May butted in, "the special relationship exists only between the United States and the United Kingdom because of our shared history."

"We have no special relationship because you will kill us all!" Kim called out.

Turning around, Trump asked his Chief of Staff: "Is this guy from North Korea?"

"No, he's the South Korean President," Priebus replied.

"So, why does he think we're going to kill him?"

"I don't know, Sir."

Sighing, Trump said: "Get me a translator, Reince."

While Kim gasped, Priebus said: "I'm not sure we'll be able to get a Korean translator at such short notice on a Sunday."

"I don't care what language he speaks, as long as he's the best translator in Washington," Trump replied.

As Priebus left the Oval Office, Kim said sharply: "You wrote: 'Doom and gloom for North Korea! South, East and West!'"

"And?" he said disinterestedly, while practising his signature.

Aghast, Kim turned to May for support, and she asked: "So, are you planning to bomb the entire Korean Peninsula?"

"No, only south, east and west North Korea, as I said," Trump replied. "I've decided to spare the north of North Korea because part of that region borders Russia."

Surprised, his guests looked at each other. "Well, that seems like a rather sensible approach," May said. "You don't want to anger the Russian bear – you can't trust the Russians."

"I am very, very good friends with Vladimir Putin and all the other Russians in the world," Trump said, eyeing her coldly. "They are very, very good people who have done a tremendous amount for me – a tremendous amount."

"I was only joking," she said, and chuckled nervously. "I do think it's a splendid idea."

"But it's an expensive operation," Trump replied. "The United States can't afford it, so the UK will have to pay for it."

Gasping, May meekly said: "But Mr President…"

"Because of the special relationship between our countries."

Sitting up straight, she cleared her voice and said: "Mr President, it would be an honour for the UK to pay for this war."

"And by the way, the Scottish Government wants me to pay a fine because they say the work we've done at my golf course near Aberdeen has damaged the surrounding dunes, but I won't pay it."

"That's an issue for the Scottish Government," May said, relieved.

"Only a weak Prime Minister would say that. A powerful leader would sort this out."

"I'll look into it as soon as I get back to London," she said. "I'm sure it's just a misunderstanding."

"Let's hope so for the sake of your career. Remember: ask not what your country can do for you – ask what you can do for our country." Then he practised his signature again and said: "I've got work to do now."

Baffled, Kim and May looked at each other. Turning to their host again, the former said testily: "Excuse me, I want the full picture!"

"Me too," May said anxiously. "I was hoping we could pose together for the photographers outside."

"There are photographers outside?" Trump asked, looking up.

"Yes, they're on the lawn," she said excitedly.

Dropping his pen, he said: "Then let's go and have our picture taken." Looking at Kim, he added: "The full picture, as you say."

While the South Korean President gasped once more, Trump led his visitors out into the cold and onto the South Lawn. As they headed down the short path from the Oval Office, Kim tried to say something, but Trump ignored him and May subtly pushed him out of the way until they were in full view of the photographers and he gave up.

When the three leaders posed for the cameras, a journalist shouted: "How did your talks go, Mr President?"

"They went incredibly well," Trump replied, and gave the reporters a thumbs-up. "The best talks ever."

"Are the UK and South Korea supporting your war against North Korea?" another journalist asked.

"Only the United Kingdom," May said, as the cameras kept clicking. "That's because we have a special relationship with the United States, and I am very pleased that our countries have such a special relationship."

"Maggie is a very, very good friend – the best," Trump said. "She and I go back a long time."

"Theresa," she whispered to him, and chuckled nervously.

"Yes, it's like a freezer – very cold day today," he replied, and shivered to stress the point. But hearing the cameras, he smiled again, grabbed her hand and held it up as though awarding her a boxing title.

"So, this joint war effort is a sign that the special relationship between our two countries still exists?" a British journalist asked.

"Yes, it's very, very special," Trump replied, and smiled indulgently while patting May's hand. Then he dropped his smile as well as her hand, shivered again and said: "Gosh, it's freezing!" And with a pat on Kim's back and a wave to the press corps, he returned to the Oval Office, where he sat down behind his desk and tweeted: "It's freezing in DC – we need global warming!"

As 2pm in Washington and Monday 3am in Pyongyang approached, the President was joined by Chief Strategist

Steve Bannon, White House Chief of Staff Reince Priebus, Press Secretary Sean Spicer, Secretary of Defense Jim Mattis, the Chairman of the Joint Chiefs of Staff, Joe Dunford, and the Chief of Staff of the Army, Mark Milley.

Mattis and the two generals had prepared an intelligence report for Trump, and handing over the file marked "Top Secret", he said: "Sir, if you're sticking to the 3am start for the attack, you will have to decide if that's Korean time or our time or any other time zone."

Dumping Mattis' folder on his desk without looking at it, Trump said: "I want to start as soon as possible, so let's take the earliest option."

"That's Korean time, which means we would attack in five minutes."

"Then let's nuke the Vietcong!" he gleefully exclaimed.

Looking at his watch, Milley said: "We need more time to prepare."

"Then pick another time zone," Trump said impatiently.

"Sir," Dunford said, "we think you should read our intelligence report first before you launch a nuclear strike. The world would suffer greatly from nuclear war."

"I don't care about the world," he snapped. "I care about America – I want to make America great again."

"So do we, but by using nuclear weapons against North Korea, you will potentially kill millions of people in South Korea, China and Russia, too," Mattis said. Nodding towards the file on the desk, he added: "It's all in our report."

Stepping forward, Bannon took the folder and said: "Gentlemen, the President is an audio-visual learner – he won't read the report."

"It's very short," Dunford said. "It basically just says: 'Don't do it!'"

"The President is an audio-visual learner, if you get my drift," Bannon insisted, and looked sternly at the general. "He will not read this or indeed any other report."

"I'm bored now," Trump sighed. "I thought we'd just go and nuke them, but if it's that complicated, I don't want to do it any more. I'd rather have a parrot because it'll just repeat everything I say and won't make things complicated." Turning to the Chief of Staff, he added: "Priebus, can you get me a parrot?"

"Now?" he asked, puzzled, and the three military advisers nodded eagerly.

"Yes, I need it now," he said tiredly. "The war has worn me out."

As Priebus left the Oval Office, Spicer asked: "How are we going to explain to the press that we're not going to war after all?"

"We'll just pretend we did," the President replied. "We'll say we decided against nuclear weapons but that we crossed into North Korea on Monday at 3am in whatever time zone, and we'll show them some wire mesh to prove it."

"How's that going to prove anything?" the Press Secretary asked.

"We'll say it's from the border. And we'll pay some South Koreans to dress up as North Korean soldiers, so we can parade them in front of the media and pretend we captured them."

"Hum, it's unusual, but it could work," Dunford said to his fellow military advisers, who nodded.

Thus, after Monday 3am had passed in all time zones around the globe, General Vincent K. Brooks, the Commander of the US forces in South Korea, presented two supposedly captured North Korean soldiers and several pieces of badly cut wire mesh to the baffled world media gathered for a press conference in Seoul. And while CNN and *The New York Times* questioned whether the mission had produced any tangible benefits, Breitbart declared it an unqualified success and the President tweeted "Victory!!!", before adding: "We will build a gold-plated obelisk in front of the White House to commemorate this tremendous triumph. It will be twice as big as the Washington Monument, and we'll call it the Trump Monument."

Caligula pretends to have invaded Great Britain

After a terrific start to Caligula's short reign as Rome's ruler, things quickly unravelled, epitomised by the fact that he presented his aborted invasion of Great Britain as a success by parading fake prisoners of war and displaying seashells to prove that his army had crossed the English Channel.

Born Gaius Julius Caesar Germanicus in 12AD, he became Rome's third Emperor aged twenty-four upon succeeding his late adoptive grandfather, the tyrannical Tiberius. Initially welcomed as a breath of fresh air, Caligula turned out to be even more callous than his predecessor, who'd anticipated as much, warning: "I am nursing a viper in Rome's bosom."

Caligula punished people "not necessarily for major offences, but merely for ... failing to swear by his genius", while important judgements depended "entirely on the caprice of his pen" and "anger incited him to a flood of verbiage", first-century historian Suetonius wrote.

Like Donald Trump with his infamous 'hand jerk', the Roman Emperor used polite greetings to assert his power, acknowledging the centurion Cassius Chaerea – who ultimately stabbed and killed him – by extending his middle finger for Chaerea to kiss, then "wiggled it obscenely". Caligula's narcissism arguably also provided the blueprint for Trump, who has called for global warming because "it's freezing and snowing in New York" and boasted that not getting a sexual disease was "my personal Vietnam" and made him "feel like a great and very brave soldier". Caligula, on the other hand, complained about "how bad the times were" because "the prosperity of his own reign would lead to its being wholly forgotten, and he often prayed for a great military catastrophe or for famine, plague, fire or at least an earthquake."

When none of these auspicious events occurred, he took matters into his own hands and "wasted no time" to collect "military supplies on an unprecedented scale". Yet, after moving his troops into position on the English Channel, he didn't ask them to invade Great Britain but instead told them to gather seashells, which he presented in Rome to prove that his army had crossed the strait. As further proof for the successful invasion, he also paraded French slaves as POWs, then had a lighthouse built to commemorate his famous victory.

Given that Caligula also wanted to be treated like a god and arranged "for the most revered or artistically famous statues of the gods" to have "their heads replaced by his own", it is perhaps not surprising that he rubbed some folk up the wrong way. Less than four years after becoming Emperor, he was murdered, with many high-profile people said to have been either directly involved in, or at least aware of, the plot to assassinate him.

Further reading:

Caligula by Suetonius

"History: Caligula (AD 12 – 41)", BBC: http://bbc.in/2yk02MO

CHAPTER TWO
Changing times

At 4.22 Eastern time on Tuesday morning, the President switched on the lights in the Oval Office, scratched his backside and went over to the bird cage on the antique wooden chest of drawers by the Georgian windows to say hello to his sleepy blue-fronted Amazon parrot. Then he sat down behind his desk and took to Twitter to share the lessons learnt during his first few days in office.

"Our incredibly successful North Korea campaign proved that our military is the best again," he wrote. "Unlike under Barack Obama – or Osama Obama as I prefer to call him because he cares more about Muslims than the United States! #public_enemy"

Even at this early hour, lots of people all over the world – from Kentucky to Nebraska and Wyoming – immediately liked his tweet. Meanwhile, Trump added: "Now we need to build on that success, and we'll start off by changing the number of days in a week from 7 to 12."

Then he posted another message explaining: "There are 12 inches in a foot, so why not 12 weekdays? It will increase productivity and make America great again! The change is effective immediately."

An hour and a half later, just as he was scratching his behind after returning to the Oval Office from the toilet, he received a call from Sean Spicer, who anxiously said: "Mr President, please don't do this!"

"Do what?" Trump replied, and kept scratching as he sat down on his high-back leather executive chair.

"Don't change the number of weekdays! It'll backfire."

"No, it won't. It will be great for the economy because people will have to work twice as many days to have a weekend off, so we'll double our productivity."

Confused, the White House Press Secretary hesitated, then said: "Maybe run it by Steve Mnuchin – I'm not very good at math."

"Spicer, I'm worth ten billion dollars, I don't need any help with math," Trump snapped. "I promised the voters that I'd create more work, and now I'm delivering on that promise."

As soon as he realised that that's what he was doing, he tweeted: "By introducing longer weeks, I am delivering on my promise to create more work – something Osama Obama didn't manage in eight years!"

"I think the voters probably thought you wanted to create more work for people who are unemployed," Spicer said. "People who have jobs usually want to work less."

"Then let's cut the hours in a day to twelve instead of twenty-four – like that, we can reduce the hours people work every day to four or five and still be as productive," Trump replied, and told his Twitter followers about the change.

Panicking, Spicer said: "You can't just change the hours in a day."

"Why not?"

"Because …" he said, and tried to think of a reason. "Because all other countries around the world have twenty-four-hour days."

"Then we should definitely change it because I hate globalisation," Trump replied. "Plus, it will stimulate our economy because we'll have to produce new digital clocks and watches."

"I guess so," Spicer said uncertainly.

"Let me call Mnuchin to see what he thinks."

Half an old-style hour later, the Treasury Secretary arrived at the Oval Office and was told about the new measures.

"Those decisions will make America great again, right?" Trump said, and scrutinised his face.

Shifting uncomfortably in his chair on the other side of the presidential desk, Mnuchin hesitated, then said: "Well, it's quite unusual."

"So, you think I made a mistake?" Trump asked, alarmed.

"No, I didn't mean that," he said quickly. "We wanted to shake things up, and this is the way to do it."

"I'm so glad you think that," Trump said, relieved. "It's a great idea, isn't it?"

"Absolutely."

"You have to think bigly to be successful."

"I agree, and to be honest, it already sounds kind of outdated to me to have a seven-day week and twenty-four hours in a day."

"Twenty-four hours is for losers," the President said. "Twelve hours feels right." Scratching his bottom again, he added: "Your opinion is very important to me, Mnuchin, because I trust you more than anybody else."

"Thank you, Sir," he replied humbly, while trying to suppress a smile.

"We'll double our productivity because everyone will have to work twice as long to get a weekend off," Trump said excitedly.

Mnuchin opened his mouth, but noticing that the President was closely watching him, he bit his tongue, then said: "Yes, Sir."

"I knew it!" he exclaimed, beaming. "Spicer said my math was wrong, but you don't become as rich as I am if you can't add up. Do you know how much money I've got, my munchkin?"

"Five billion dollars," he said eagerly. "I read your entry in the *Forbes* billionaires list."

"It's ten billion!" Trump called out, banging his fist on the desk. "They lied!" And while Mnuchin apologised profusely, he turned to his computer and tweeted: "Never believe anything that Forbes says – they are the enemy of the American people!!!"

The Treasury Secretary hastily took his phone out of his pocket and liked the tweet. Seeing this endorsement just as he scratched his bottom, the President said: "I trust you, Mnuchin, and that's why I'm going to tell you something I haven't told anyone, not even my wife. As you know, I am officially the healthiest President ever. But lately, I'm having trouble when I'm trying to, you know…"

Puzzled, Mnuchin looked at him. "Sorry, Sir, I don't know what you mean."

"Well, it's difficult for me to, you know…" he said, grimacing as he scratched harder.

"To masturbate?"

"Not to masturbate!" he exclaimed. "Jesus, I am the President of the United States – if I want to have sex with a woman, I'll just grab her by the pussy!"

"Grab her by the pussy!" his parrot said.

"I was talking about wiping my ass."

"Grab her by the pussy!" the parrot repeated.

"You've lost me, Sir," Mnuchin said.

"Well, these days, I find it harder to clean myself after I've used the bathroom, so my ass gets itchy and I keep scratching it," he explained, while demonstrating the issue.

"Oh," Mnuchin said, disconcerted as he paid attention to what his boss was doing.

"But I trust you, which is why I've chosen you."

"I beg your pardon."

Sighing, the President rose and removed his hand from his backside as he went over to the other side of the desk, before placing it on Mnuchin's shoulder and looking straight into his eyes. "I need someone to wipe my butt for me when I go to the bathroom, so that I don't end up scratching it all the time," he said. "That's not very statesman-like."

Panicking, Mnuchin said: "Sir, I'm not sure I'm the right person for that job."

"Yes, you are," Trump reassured him. "I need someone I can fully trust, and I trust you more than anybody else." Tightening his grip on Mnuchin's shoulder, he added: "It's a sign of my respect for you."

"Thank you, Sir," he replied nervously.

Patting Mnuchin's cheek with the hand he wouldn't have to use for scratching any longer, Trump said: "It's a great honour for you. Do you feel flattered?"

"Yes, Sir."

"Tremendous," Trump said, and sat down on his chair again. "Your new job title is Presidential Ass Assistant," he added, and started typing to announce the appointment on Twitter.

"Sir, I'd be very grateful if we could avoid making that an official job title and telling people about my new role!"

"Why?" Trump asked, frowning at the Treasury Secretary while his hands hovered over the keyboard. "Are you embarrassed?"

"No, not at all. If I was embarrassed, I'd just say it like I'm stuttering – Presidential Ass... Assistant. But I don't see any reason to be embarrassed. I just prefer to be humble and modest about it, in the same way that you're humble and modest about being President of the United States."

Trump considered this for a moment, then nodded, deleted the words he'd written and said: "I'm pleased to hear that my attitude is rubbing off on you." Then his phone began to ring and didn't stop for several hours.

That day, Mnuchin was thrown in at the deep end as the vitriolic criticism from all sides for the President's time-management measures caused him to visit the lavatory more often than usual. Finally, at about eleven o'clock in the morning, it was all getting too much for Trump and he decided to escape to Mar-a-Lago, his members-only resort in Florida.

Looking at the Atlantic Ocean and the palm trees below as the Air Force One flew into Palm Beach International Airport, he breathed a sigh of relief and tweeted: "Looking forward to getting away from the chaos in Washington and spending a whole week at Mar-a-Lago. See you back at the White House in 12 days!"

But ten minutes later, once his presidential state car and the attendant police escort had crossed the long highway bridge connecting the mainland to the narrow barrier island that was home to his 1920s mansion, he saw that chaos had followed him from the capital. Hundreds of angry people were lining the extensive perimeter of his property, holding up placards, pointing at him and shouting abuse.

Shaken by his subjects' open dissent, Trump avoided the members upon arrival at his club, which the marketing literature described as "tremendous" and "the best" because it combined the most opulent features of any old architectural style the interior designer had ever heard of. Rushing through the gold-flavoured lobby towards the lifts to escape to his penthouse, he was intercepted by a man he'd never met before.

"Mr President, I'm Dennis Wardlow, the mayor of Palm Beach," the man said. "I need to talk to you."

"Not now, I'm busy," Trump replied, and continued walking towards the gold-plated lifts, while secret service agents swarmed across the lobby.

"Sir," the mayor said, hurrying after him, "each time you're visiting Palm Beach – which seems to be all the time – our local businesses have to shut because of security concerns. They've already lost hundreds of thousands of dollars, and if you're now introducing a twelve-day week, you'll damage our tourist industry even more because there'll be fewer weekends."

"I am pro-business," Trump replied, as he pressed the lift button. "A seven-day week might be good for the tourist shops here, but it damages our economy. And anyway, the club members prefer to have fewer tourists around in Palm Beach."

Gobsmacked, Wardlow stared at the President while the lift doors opened. "As mayor of this town, the preferences of Mar-a-Lago's members are irrelevant to me if they are not aligned with the needs of our local community," he snapped, while Trump stepped inside the lift. Moving towards the President until a secret service agent grabbed his arm and held him back, he angrily added: "If you ignore our concerns, then we'll secede from the United States!"

"Throw this man out of the club," Trump said to the agent, and put his key in to activate the golden button for his penthouse.

"We will declare independence and establish the Palm Beach Republic!" Wardlow shouted, and was escorted off the premises.

Once inside his rococo-on-speed-style penthouse, the President immediately called the Treasury Secretary.

"The voters treat me very, very unfairly!"

"I know!" Mnuchin said, delighted about the call. "I just saw it on TV. It's very, very unfair."

"You shouldn't believe the media – it's fake news."

Unsure how to respond to this catch-22, Mnuchin hesitated.

"I want you to come to Florida and see for yourself," Trump added. "They behave like children, and we need to stop it."

Just over three hours later, at 5.30 in the afternoon, the Treasury Secretary arrived at Mar-a-Lago and, after carrying out his new task, asked the President to turn back the clock.

"People aren't ready for your changes yet," he said, as they sat down on either side of the gold-plated desk in Trump's penthouse. "They don't understand what you're trying to do because you're a visionary. It's the difference between having ten billion dollars and being poor."

"People are poor, stupid and unfair," Trump said, but felt a bit better. "You're the only person in the world I can trust, Mnuchin." As the latter suppressed a smile, he added: "So, what should I do now?"

"I think it would be a good idea for you to meet the voters halfway," he replied. "If they don't understand that you're, like, really, really smart and essentially a genius, then just change things back to a seven-day week and a twenty-four-hour day."

"Are you sure?" he asked, frowning. "We'll lose half our productivity if we do that."

"Yes, but we'll still achieve one hundred per cent of our current economic output."

"One hundred per cent?" Trump asked, and his face lit up. "That's incredible!"

So, he fired up his computer, logged on to Twitter and prompted Palm Beach's mayor to reconsider his secession plans by announcing: "We're going back to a 7-day week and a 24-hour day to bring the economy up to 100% – something Osama Obama never managed!"

Cutting the number of hours in a day and lengthening the week

For hundreds of years, people with too much time on their hands have argued we should measure it in a different way. Having ousted the ruling royals at the end of the eighteenth century, the leaders of the French Revolution must have also been at a loose end because wondering what else they could oppose, they, too, homed in on the clock and the calendar. Determined to make things easier by using ten as the base for all measurements instead of having arbitrary groupings like, say, a dozen, the revolutionaries divided their French republican calendar into, er, twelve months. However, they split them equally into three *décades*, or weeks, of ten days each. And since a dozen thirty-day months meant there were a few days left over, they simply slapped those on at the end of the year like leftovers.

This system was used – ironically – for twelve years, with Napoleon reinstating the Gregorian calendar in 1806. By contrast, decimal time – which was introduced along with the French republican calendar and saw each day split into ten hours and, in turn, one hundred minutes and a hundred seconds – lasted just a year and a half and was barely used at all, partly because it cost too much to replace clocks and watches.

Further reading:

"Decimal Time: Misadventures of a Revolutionary Idea, 1793–2008" by Héctor Vera: http://bit.ly/2xbJvKy

Time and the French Revolution: The Republican Calendar, 1789-year XIV by Matthew Shaw

A small part of Florida secedes

When US authorities set up a checkpoint about thirty miles south-west of Miami in 1982 to intercept illegal immigrants, they caused huge traffic jams in and out of the Florida Keys, prompting the islands to secede and declare war against the United States.

The congestion caused genuine concerns for the local tourist industry, as many people cancelled their trips to the southern-most part of the United States. Arguing that the checkpoint on the mainland amounted to a border station and therefore implied that the federal government considered the gently arching island chain a foreign country, Key West mayor Dennis Wardlow and his supporters decided they might as well become independent. So, on 23 April, the leader of the revolution – standing on a flatbed truck in front of the Old Customs building in Key West – announced the creation of the Conch Republic and immediately declared war against the United States.

This was followed by tumultuous scenes, as the now Prime Minister Wardlow (or one of his collaborators, depending on who you believe) broke a baguette-like loaf of stale Cuban bread over the head of a navy officer, before instantly surrendering to the federal agents who'd arrived in the lead-up to the much-publicised event. He then requested a billion dollars in foreign aid from the United States "to rebuild our nation after the long federal siege", but as of 2017, the US government still hasn't paid up. However, following the Conch Republic's declaration of independence – which is celebrated for ten days each year – the US did remove its controversial checkpoint.

Having defined itself as a "state of mind", the young country adopted a foreign policy focused on "the mitigation of world tension through the exercise of humour". In 1995, it used this approach –

as well as the deployment of its baguette-like weapon of choice – to repel the US army when the 478th Civil Affairs Battalion decided to carry out an unannounced training exercise in the Keys. The Conch Republic responded to "this affront to our sovereignty" by complaining to the Pentagon, the State Department and the battalion in question. At the same time, La Dichosa Bakery went into overdrive, producing "a formidable quantity of ammunition".

Unsurprisingly, the United States soon got cold feet. At 10.50pm on Thursday 21 September, about thirty-six hours after news of the training exercise had reached Key West, the 478th battalion sent a fax saying the US army "in no way meant to challenge or impugn the sovereignty of the Conch Republic".

Reminiscing about founding the nation in April 2017, Wardlow revealed that what now sounds like a humorous historical footnote was, in fact, "very scary at the time" because some Key West citizens were so worried about the potential implication for issues such as social security that he received death threats and was told he was committing career suicide.

Further reading:

Conch Republic website: https://conchrepublic.com/

"That Time the Florida Keys Tried to Secede from the US by Dropping Conch Fritter Bombs", Munchies: http://bit.ly/2fEi4xR

Groom of the Stool

In Tudor England, there was fierce competition for places in the monarch's inner circle, with no position more coveted than that of Groom of the Stool, or royal arse-wiper. Introduced in the fifteenth century by Henry VII, this ostensibly shitty job became a prestigious post under his son, Henry VIII, offering the kind of status you'll attain today only if you have powerful friends and a PhD from Oxbridge. Given that you knew the king's backside more intimately than your own, he trusted you implicitly and often shared secrets during those cherished private moments when you watched him sit on a velvet-cushioned wooden box called a close stool, struggling with constipation due to his meat- and wine-based diet.

An added perk to the job was that when the monarch died, you inherited his close stool. However, upon acceding to the throne in 1837, Queen Victoria must have thought she'd rather pass her piss pots on to next of kin, for she abolished the position.

Further reading:

The Private Lives of the Tudors: Uncovering the Secrets of Britain's Greatest Dynasty by Tracy Borman

"The Private Lives of the Tudors: Uncovering the Secrets of Britain's Greatest Dynasty by Tracy Borman – review", *The Guardian*: http://bit.ly/1WsLWhs

CHAPTER THREE
Spinning out of control

As soon as Kellyanne Conway found out that Steve Mnuchin was in Mar-a-Lago, she was on her way to Reagan National Airport and boarded the first plane to Palm Beach.

Arriving at ten o'clock in the evening, she discovered the President and the Treasury Secretary sitting at one of the candle-lit tables on the terrace by the pool, while the other diners toasted Trump's decision to leave the basic framework of the world unchanged for now. Yet, she barely had time to say hello because her boss's mobile phone rang and his tremendous news about the one-hundred-per-cent economy was overshadowed by another incident.

"Sir, I'm afraid one of our aircraft carriers lost a nuclear bomb during our aborted invasion of North Korea," General Joe Dunford said on the other end of the line.

"That's fake news!" Trump hissed, as Conway sat down at the table. "The invasion wasn't aborted – it was incredibly successful. General Brooks presented some tremendous evidence for it."

"Yes, Sir!" the Chairman of the Joint Chiefs of Staff replied. "However, during our successful invasion of North Korea, we lost a plane armed with a nuclear device in the Yellow Sea."

Chuckling, he said: "That's very funny, General. I've had enough of political correctness, so well done for calling it the Yellow Sea."

"That's what it's called, Sir. In any case, do you have a moment to discuss this extremely sensitive information?"

"OK," Trump sighed. "Let me put you on speakerphone, so Mnuchin and Conway can hear you, as well."

"Is there anybody else with you?" Dunford asked, alarmed.

"No, just those two," he replied, as he changed the settings on his phone and put it on the table. "And the club members, of course, but I don't have any secrets from them."

"Sir, we can't discuss the loss of a nuclear bomb in front of members of the public," Dunford said, to gasps from the diners.

"Well, it's too late now – they've already heard you," Trump replied, as some guests started live-streaming the events on Facebook. "In any case, they are extremely trustworthy – I trust them more than anybody else."

Mnuchin flinched, while Dunford sighed and announced: "On Monday morning at 2.54 local time, a Rockwell B-1 Lancer armed with a B83 nuclear weapon accidentally rolled off the deck of *USS Ronald Reagan* in the Yellow Sea, approximately eighty miles west of Incheon, South Korea."

"Why were they attacking South Korea?" Trump joked, and the club members laughed.

"They were there to attack North Korea, Sir," he clarified, prompting Trump to contort his eyes and tilt his head as though disabled to suggest that Dunford was mentally impaired. "The aircraft came to rest sixteen thousand feet below the surface of the ocean, and none of the explosives on board detonated," the general continued. "According to our bomb disposal experts, an explosion is now impossible, so no one is at risk. But if news of this incident is leaked, it will likely cause a diplomatic row."

Raising his hands as though at a loss, Trump asked the audience: "What do you think we should do, folks? Should we keep this to ourselves or tell the dishonest media about it? Let's take this decision together – this is a democracy after all."

"Keep it to ourselves!" some people shouted, and others applauded.

But one middle-aged lady looked shocked and said: "You can't do that – you have to let the public know."

"You're fired!" Trump replied, and everyone laughed.

"I think we should discuss this privately," Conway said. "Let's go to your penthouse."

"Did you hear that, folks? She wants to come to my penthouse," he joked, and milked the moment as his subjects whistled approvingly. "OK, sweetheart, let's go," he said, to more laughter. Then he took his phone and the three of them headed inside, Trump turning around to his audience one last time as he smiled and added: "What happens in the penthouse stays in the penthouse."

After another round of applause, the Commander in Chief and his advisers crossed the lobby and went towards the lifts. But looking at his watch, he said: "How about the two of you talk about this on your own down here and I go upstairs? Now that we have decided not to tell anyone about the incident, my job is done."

"But Mr President," Conway said anxiously. "A lot of things happened today, so I wanted to give you my input."

"Don't worry, Mnuchin has given me some tremendous advice," he said, and stepped into the lift. "I trust him one hundred per cent."

"But Mr President..." Conway pleaded, as the doors closed and he went up to his penthouse. Turning to Mnuchin, she hissed: "You're just an ass-wiper!"

"Who told you that?" he exclaimed.

"No one told me that," she replied, baffled. "It's obvious."

"Well, I'm not," he said, and scratched his nose to check the smell of his wiping hand. "If there's anyone who tries to ingratiate themselves with the President, it's you!"

"Ha!" she sneered. "And what good does it do me?"

"Earlier on, he called you his sweetheart."

"Oh, come on – he was being totally inappropriate again and making out I wanted to have sex with him."

"Still." Frowning at her, he added: "I will watch you very closely, Kellyanne – the President doesn't need two advisers!"

Yet, five hours later, at about 4am on Wednesday morning, that theory was disproved since it was Conway rather than Mnuchin who alerted Trump to the fact that the information about the nuclear bomb had been leaked. Having stayed up all night plotting how she could replace the Treasury Secretary in the President's affection, she saw a report about the incident on CNN and immediately rang Trump, who was already awake and tweeting on his phone.

"You'll need to give a press conference to address this," she said. "It won't go down well, but if we could find some positive news to push out at the same time, maybe we can distract the media."

"I hate the media," he snapped, and banged his fist on his gold-plated desk. "They are out of control, and they treat me very, very unfairly."

"They're like sharks, so we need to give them some positive news to feed on so they'll stop focusing on the stupid nuclear bomb."

"How about Mar-a-Lago?" Trump said, as he swivelled around in his high-back leather executive chair and looked out of the window into the dark beyond the pool. "This is such a tremendous place. Isn't this place tremendous?"

"It's a lovely place," she agreed.

"So, we should focus on that."

"Well," she said uncertainly, "to really distract the press, we'd probably need some other good news to go with it."

"OK, I trust you on that," he said, and turned around again. "I trust you more than anybody else."

"Thank you, Sir," she said, and tried to suppress a smile. "How about we invite another head of state to join you here? Someone who's popular, so that it reflects well on you and Mar-a-Lago."

"That's a great idea," he said excitedly. "What about that guy who's doing bigly?"

"Who's that?"

"You know the one I mean," he said impatiently. "The one who's always on TV because he's popular and Canadian."

"Prime Minister Trudeau?"

"Trudeau was Canada's Prime Minister in the seventies," he sneered. "His wife used to be in the news all the time because she was a groupie and incredibly hot. She was tremendous – very young."

"And their son is Canada's Prime Minister now."

"Really? I'll call him now, then, and tell him to come here for an emergency meeting."

"It's too early to call him. Call him after seven."

Grumbling, he switched on his laptop. "No wonder Canada's economy is doing so much worse than ours if their head of state gets up so late."

Hearing the sound of Windows starting up, Conway said: "Please don't tweet that!"

"Why not?"

"Because he probably won't come here if you do."

Sighing, Trump said: "OK, I won't mention him."

Then they hung up and he tweeted: "Heads of North American countries who get up very, very late should not be surprised that their economy is doing so much worse than ours!"

As Mexico's President condemned Trump's latest apparent dig at his country, Trudeau was informed about the nuclear incident.

He therefore put two and two together when he was summoned to an emergency meeting, so he readily agreed to fly from Toronto to Palm Beach, his arrival at Mar-a-Lago expected for noon. Meanwhile, Trump went to face the press on the terrace by the pool at 8am, with Conway and Mnuchin standing behind him.

As journalists from around the world scrambled to put their microphones as close to him as possible, a CNN reporter asked: "Mr President, is there a chance that the nuclear bomb that was lost during your failed invasion of North Korea might explode?"

"The invasion didn't fail – it was incredibly successful," he replied. "And by the way, we're going to build a memorial at the White House and it's going to be tremendous, believe me."

"But what about the nuclear bomb?" a *New York Times* journalist asked.

"General Dunford told me last night that the story was made up by fake media outlets like CNN and *The New York Times*."

"But in the video that was posted on Facebook, you and General Dunford said that a nuclear bomb had been lost in the Yellow Sea," the reporter insisted.

Puzzled, Trump turned around to Conway and Mnuchin, who both looked confused. But then the Treasury Secretary stepped forward and said: "It's just a misunderstanding."

"It's just a misunderstanding, folks," Trump agreed, and gave him a thumbs-up, prompting Conway to scowl at Mnuchin. "Instead of getting all worked up about it, we should enjoy the fact that we're in Mar-a-Lago. Isn't this place tremendous, folks?"

"It's the best," Mnuchin said, and received another angry look.

"There you go, folks – it's the best," Trump said. "And Canada's Prime Minister is coming here this afternoon, so it's going to be tremendous."

Baffled, the journalists looked at each other. "Trudeau is coming here?" one of them asked.

"Yes," he replied, smiling indulgently. "I know you guys love him because he's a tremendous guy and his mother used to be a groupie. I would have dated her back in the seventies, but unfortunately, I never met her."

And thus, the media had a new story to focus on.

A few hours later, Canada's Prime Minister was driven onto the premises, his serious demeanour reflecting his concern about the loss of a nuclear bomb so close to a heavily populated region.

Already waiting on the terrace by the pool as Trudeau and his security detail walked along the path that divided the impeccably manicured lawn, Trump put on the solemn presidential game face that had worked so well during his first meeting with foreign dignitaries. Stony-faced, he watched his opponent approach. When Trudeau reached the terrace, Trump's right lower arm went up at a ninety-degree angle, but he kept his upper arm firmly aligned with his body so that the Canadian Prime Minister was forced to move in towards him for a handshake and he could push and pull him all over the place.

Yet, Trudeau's grip was too firm for the President to subdue him. So, instead he whacked his back with his left hand while smiling in a friendly way before squeezing the younger man's cheek as though he was a little boy.

"Great to see you," Trump said, still smiling as he ushered him towards the two gold-plated chairs his staff had moved outside for his planned photo opportunity.

After they'd been sitting and smiling for the cameras for an absurd amount of time, Trudeau leaned in towards Trump and whispered: "Shall we go inside and start our meeting now?"

"Just keep smiling," he replied, and patted the Prime Minister's hand for the cameras.

"Who of the two of you do you think is better looking, Mr President?" a tabloid journalist joked.

"I am," he said, to laughter, which went up a notch when he added: "Trudeau would be better looking if I'd met his mother in the seventies, when she was a groupie." Turning to his guest, he asked: "She must be quite old now, right?"

"She's two years younger than you," he coolly replied.

"Yeah, I thought so."

"So, why have you come to Mar-a-Lago, Prime Minister?" another journalist asked.

"Because Canada is such a cold country and this is such a tremendous place," Trump said on his behalf. "He wanted to enjoy a bit of sunshine and play some golf, so I said, 'Why don't you come down to Mar-a-Lago and we play a few rounds at my golf club?', which, by the way, is the best golf club in the world."

Puzzled, Trudeau turned to him, and an equally baffled reporter asked: "But you'll discuss the loss of the nuclear weapon, right?"

"We don't want to talk about that," Trump said. "It's such a beautiful day, and we don't want to ruin it, especially considering that we're at Mar-a-Lago, which many of the greatest experts in the world – some very, very special people who I've personally met many, many times – have called the most tremendous place in the world."

"Could I speak to you in private for a moment?" Trudeau asked, and rose.

"Sure," Trump replied. Getting up, he said to the press contingent: "Folks, we're going inside now to catch up before we go and play golf."

When they were in the gold-flavoured foyer, Trudeau glared at him and asked: "Is this 'emergency meeting' some kind of publicity stunt?"

"No," Trump said, surprised. "It's to promote Mar-a-Lago."

"You're kidding, right?" His mouth open and his hands placed on his hips, he scrutinised the President's face. "What about the nuclear bomb?"

"Let's just forget about it. Apparently, it's not going to explode anyway."

Gobsmacked, Trudeau stared at him for a moment, then stormed off without another word, taking the already bewildered press corps by even greater surprise as he returned to his car and was driven back to Palm Beach International Airport.

Rushing into the lobby closely followed by Mnuchin, Conway anxiously asked: "What happened?"

"He just left without any explanation," Trump said.

"No wonder that Canada's economy is doing so much worse than ours if their head of state is so flaky," Mnuchin said.

"I totally agree," Trump replied, earning the Treasury Secretary an annoyed look from Conway. "He's a bad person – he's treated me very, very unfairly."

"Well, let's think of a plan B," Conway said. "How about you meet some ordinary voters here in Florida for a photo op?"

"What do you think, Mnuchin?" he asked. "I could shake hands with a few club members in front of the press."

"I meant ordinary people," she said. "People who aren't rich."

"The club members aren't rich," he snapped. "I'm richer than all of them!"

"You're worth ten billion dollars," Mnuchin said.

"That's right: Ten. Billion. Dollars."

"Yes, Sir," Conway said, and scowled at Mnuchin. "But I meant people who are even poorer than the club members. Some real rednecks."

"People like that aren't allowed inside the club."

"I was thinking you could go and meet them where they live, and then we'll get the press to take pictures of you with those people to make you seem folksy. And maybe you can help them in some way to make it look like you care about them."

"What do you think, Mnuchin?" Trump asked uncertainly.

"I don't know," the Treasury Secretary said, as he and Conway eyed each other. "It might actually be a good idea," he reluctantly conceded.

"So, where should we go?" the President asked.

"There's a place called Homestead Base near Miami that is among the poorest communities in Florida,"

Conway said excitedly. "It also has an air force base, so you can shake hands with some servicemen. And Homestead sounds kind of poor, so it would be perfect."

"Sounds perfect," he replied, prompting her to smile smugly at the Treasury Secretary. "What do you think, Mnuchin?" he added.

"I think we should go to a place I've heard about called Medley," he replied, and glanced at Conway. "It's also near Miami and poor."

"Let's go there, then," Trump said. "I trust you, Mnuchin."

Flabbergasted, Conway pleaded: "But Mr President, there's an air force base in Homestead and the name sounds kind of poor!"

However, the decision had been made, and a short while later, the three of them set off in the presidential state car, trailed by secret service agents and the media.

While their convoy passed through some affluent areas as they headed south on Highway One, Mnuchin said: "About twenty per cent of Medley's residents live below the poverty line."

"So, only eighty per cent of them could afford the membership fee at Mar-a-Lago," the President deduced.

"I don't think any of them could afford it," he said. "The average household income in the town is half the average US household income."

"What does that mean?"

"It means that the average family in Medley earns twenty-five thousand dollars a year. But the Mar-a-Lago membership costs two hundred thousand dollars a year. So, the average family in Medley would have to not spend a single dollar for eight years for just one family member to afford a year's membership at your club."

"Then they should focus on getting basics like food and clothes and a nice car instead," the President said. "Why save money to become a member at Mar-a-Lago if you can't afford it?"

"You're absolutely right," Mnuchin said.

"I'll explain that to them."

"Please don't do that," Conway said. "In fact, I think it would be best if you don't talk about Mar-a-Lago at all."

"And how am I meant to promote the club if I don't talk about it?"

His aides looked at each other. "Well, these people can't afford the membership fee anyway, so just ask them what other concerns in life they have because the media will like that sort of question," the Treasury Secretary suggested.

"OK, Mnuchin, I trust you," he replied. And for once, even Conway was grateful for it.

About an hour later, the convoy arrived at Medley, less than ten miles north-west of Miami, and the President shook hands with some locals in the centre of the bleak and dusty town, with two dozen media outlets covering the encounter.

"So," Trump said to a middle-aged man, while smiling for the cameras. "What other concerns in life do you have besides the membership fee?"

Puzzled, the man looked at him. "We don't pay a membership fee – we just live here."

"So, you don't have any other concerns?"

"Well, there's a big problem round here with Burmese pythons because they kill people's dogs and cats and the wildlife in the Everglades. There are thousands of them now, and it keeps getting worse."

"Then we'll get rid of them," the President said. Addressing the journalists, he declared: "I hereby launch a program to get rid of all the Burmese pythons in the Everglades."

"But it's impossible to find them all," a local reporter pointed out. "How are you going to do that?"

"With money. People do anything for money, and they'll find those snakes if we give them enough money for it, believe me."

"A pet Burmese python costs three hundred dollars," said a rough-looking man wearing a dirty T-shirt, jeans and a stained trucker's baseball cap. Exhaling cigarette smoke, he added: "So, if you want us to get rid of them, you'll have to pay us at least the same amount."

"The government will pay five hundred dollars for each dead Burmese python," Trump instantly replied. And solemnly, he repeated: "A five-hundred-dollar reward for each dead Burmese python you deliver to the authorities here in Medley."

And while he revelled in the fact that he'd solved the voters' problem, the rough-looking man and several other people left for the nearby Everglades to catch Burmese pythons and start breeding them on an industrial scale.

"We just lost a hydrogen bomb..."

Plane crashes caused by engine failure or bad weather are the main reason why the list of nuclear near-misses is alarmingly long. Yet some incidents that almost led to disaster were so absurd, scriptwriters for *The Three Stooges* might have rejected similar plots as too slapstick.

For instance, in December 1965, at the height of the Cold War, soldiers aboard a US aircraft carrier about eighty miles away from the Japanese Ryukyu Islands briefly took their eye off the ball, resulting in a jet armed with a hydrogen bomb rolling gently off the deck and into the Pacific before coming to rest at the bottom of the ocean. Aside from the unease such a moment of distraction might cause, the faux-pas was a sensitive issue because the ship was on its way to a base in Japan, which had banned nuclear weapons after the United States had flattened the cities of Hiroshima and Nagasaki during the final days of World War II. The fact that the aircraft carrier had earlier been on combat duty in Vietnam – where the US was stepping up its controversial war effort at the time – also didn't put a positive spin on things given that Washington had never admitted to having nuclear weapons in South East Asia.

The Pentagon therefore decided to brush the incident under the carpet until 1981, when it was mentioned in passing in a nuclear-weapons accident report. However, in May 1989, towards the end of the Cold War but still before the fall of the Berlin Wall and the collapse of the Soviet Union, *Newsweek* highlighted the incident again and US officials were forced to admit that the hydrogen bomb had been lost much closer to land than five hundred miles away, as they had previously claimed. This caused outrage in Japan, but the Pentagon quickly reassured the public that the Douglas A-4 Skyhawk's cargo "posed no danger" at its final resting place.

Likewise, there is "no current or future possibility of a nuclear explosion" with regard to the hydrogen bomb dropped into the Wassaw Sound off Savannah, Georgia, on 5 February 1958 after a mid-air collision during a training exercise to simulate the use of such a weapon. The search for the device – which has never been found – had to be abandoned just a few weeks later, when another nuclear bomb was accidentally dropped only about a hundred and seventy miles further north. Flying in a B-47 Stratojet over South Carolina on 11 March 1958, Air Force Captain Bruce Kulka accidentally pulled the emergency release pin and looked on in horror as the bomb fell fifteen thousand feet into the woods at Mars Bluff. Luckily, its fission core was stored separately. Yet loaded with a large amount of traditional explosives, the bomb still injured several people, destroyed a house and created a huge crater that is now a tourist site.

Further reading:

"U.S. confirms '65 loss of H-bomb near Japanese islands", *The Washington Post:* http://wapo.st/2xSLkLg

"That One Time America Accidentally Dropped a Nuke on South Carolina", HuffPost: http://bit.ly/2hHXlO7

"Long-Missing H-Bomb A Risk?", CBS News: http://cbsn.ws/2yjUxh5

U.S. Navy and U.S. Marine Corps Aircraft Damaged or Destroyed During the Vietnam War. Volume 1: Listed by Ship Attached and By Squadron by Douglas E. Campbell

Trudeau's mum meets the Rolling Stones

When Keith Richards was busted by policemen dressed as waiters at Toronto's Harbour Castle Hotel in early 1977, they found not only a small stash of heroin but also made a much more awkward discovery outside the rooms where he and the other Rolling Stones were staying. Dressed in a bathrobe, Margaret Trudeau, the wife of Canadian Prime Minister Pierre Trudeau, was wandering up and down the hallway because she and Ronnie Wood were, according to Richards, "hitting it off really well".

The parents of Canada's current Prime Minister Justin Trudeau had been fifty-one and twenty-two, respectively, when they'd married, and were celebrating their sixth wedding anniversary just as the Rolling Stones rolled into town. "The power and the flower child" Richards calls the couple in his autobiography, writing: "She was a groupie, that's all she was, pure and simple. Nothing wrong with that. But you shouldn't be a prime minister's wife if you want to be a groupie."

To escape the publicity that came with being "a Stones appendage", Margaret flew to New York, where Mick Jagger was heading, too, leading to rumours they were having a fling, as well. The Trudeaus separated that year and Margaret became a fixture on the dancefloor at the world-famous Manhattan nightclub Studio 54. She had affairs with the likes of *Love Story* actor Ryan O'Neal and Jack Nicholson, who was "half-interested" and "left her feeling humiliated", according to *The Washington Post*.

All the while, she kept professing her love for Pierre. Yet, although they remained friends, they finally divorced in 1984, shortly before he retired from politics later that year, making him the first Canadian Prime Minister to be a single parent.

Further reading:

Life by Keith Richards

"Justin Trudeau's mother, Margaret, was like the Princess Diana of Canada —
with a happy ending", *The Washington Post:* http://wapo.st/2fKodwq

The Cobra Effect

Known to eat leopards back home in South East Asia, Burmese pythons
have put alligators and full-grown deer on the menu since they were
– intentionally or accidentally – released in the Everglades in the
late 1970s. Though it's difficult to say exactly how many of them
there are in south Florida, over two thousand have been caught,
which suggests that one of the world's largest snakes is now firmly
established at the top of the local food chain.

As a result, some native animals have almost disappeared, with
the populations of both opossums and raccoons falling by about
ninety-nine per cent within just a few years. Yet, according to
researchers Professor Michael Dorcas of North Carolina's
Davidson College and Dr John Willson of Virginia Tech, the demise
of those animals can't just be blamed on the sudden appearance
of snakes the size of which hadn't been seen in North America for
millions of years – it is also down to the prey species being too "naïve".

The same could be said of the governors in nineteenth-century
British India, who, in an attempt to rid Delhi of cobras, apparently
decided to handsomely reward those who could prove that they'd killed
one of the snakes. Quicker on the uptake than their colonial rulers,
some locals realised that breeding cobras to kill them had suddenly
become a profitable business, prompting the late German economist

Horst Siebert to coin the term "cobra effect" in 2001 to describe similarly unintended consequences of supposedly beneficial policies.

The story goes that when the British cottoned on to the fact that the number of snakes wasn't falling despite the many dead ones that were handed in, they scrapped the reward. And without a financial incentive, the Hindu 'hunters' did what anyone whose religion prohibits them from harming animals would do and set the snakes free, thereby making the infestation much worse than it had been.

The British Library's "Untold Lives" blog sets the events in the southern Indian city of Bangalore rather than Delhi, dates them to 1873 and claims a Dr Edward Nicholson implemented the 'cash for snakes' policy. Having concluded that insignificant rewards had no effect while a greater financial incentive meant that "cobras will be sought for in distant places and kept alive until required for the market", he apparently suggested to just leave the locals to it and let them "kill cobras or not as they pleased".

Further reading:

"Destruction of Venomous Snakes in India" on the British Library's "Untold Lives" blog: http://bit.ly/2yEbuyP

"Self-defeating regulation" by Patrick Walker, HeinOnline: http://bit.ly/2xPnJcC

CHAPTER FOUR
The killer rabbit

"This is insane!" Donald Trump exclaimed, on the first occasion during his presidency when insanity didn't come into it. Using his putter, he tried to bat away the flies that were buzzing around him on the third green during his solitary round on this Thursday morning at Trump International Golf Club in West Palm Beach. Then he angrily implored his caddy Steve Mnuchin: "For Christ's sake, do something to get them off me!"

As the Treasury Secretary frantically waved his hands and thereby almost ruined the Commander in Chief's carefully coiffured comb-over, the latter looked at his other caddie, Kellyanne Conway, and sneered: "Honey, you just keep standing there doing nothing while my munchkin and I deal with the flies." Yet, just as she started flapping her arms, too, he added: "Actually, I just realised how we'll get rid of them. Go and get me some honey!"

A few minutes later, Conway returned from the clubhouse with a pot of honey and offered it to Trump after he'd fired off his first shot at the fourth hole.

"You're not supposed to give it to me – you're meant to put it on Mnuchin," he snapped.

"How do you mean, Sir?" Conway asked, puzzled.

Panicking, the Treasury Secretary said: "But they're flies, not bees."

"It'll work, believe me," Trump replied. Turning to Conway, he added: "Put it on his face, so that the flies attack him, not me."

"But Mr President..." Mnuchin meekly protested, while Conway took the lid off the pot and used the spoon inside to gleefully apply a generous layer of honey to his face.

As soon as the sticky stuff covered his aide's large forehead and cheeks, the flies did indeed leave Trump alone and fell into the presidential trap before realising their mistake and ripping at Mnuchin's skin in their futile attempts to break free.

"That's better," Trump sighed, while the Treasury Secretary was blinking uncontrollably even though the distressed flies were at least half an inch away from his eyes. Then the President turned around, and unperturbed by any insects, he led his caddies from the tree-lined tee towards his ball on the fairway.

Suddenly, there was a commotion in the shrubs beneath the trees to their left, and before they'd even registered where the rustling and the agitated sounds came from, a rabbit shot out of the thicket towards them and ran straight into Mnuchin, who tripped and knocked over his boss.

Shocked as he was lying on the grass, the President stared at the animal, which made strange hissing noises and gnashed its teeth. Surrounded by three humans, the rabbit looked for an escape route, and possibly confused by the carrot-like appearance of the orange digit, it bit Trump's index finger, taking out a tiny piece of flesh. Yet instantly, it spat it out again like Mike Tyson before running off just as a well-groomed hound emerged from the shrubs to the left and a man could be heard shouting for his dog somewhere in the distance.

As the President screamed in agony, Conway immediately tended to him, while the Treasury Secretary launched himself at the approaching dog, which got distracted from the rabbit by his honey-covered face and started licking it with a vengeance.

"The fucking rabbit ate my finger!" Trump exclaimed, and held up his hand for Conway to examine the small wound. Meanwhile, she took a tissue from her purse and cleaned off the blood before giving Trump another tissue for him to wrap around his finger.

While Mnuchin pushed away the dog, got up and used his sleeve to wipe the mix of canine saliva and honey off his face, Conway turned her attention to the tiny piece of presidential flesh lying in the grass. Picking it up with another clean tissue, she showed it to Trump and said: "The rabbit spat out your finger."

"Bullshit!" he snapped, and seemed to have forgotten all about the pain. "That's the finest meat he'll ever get."

"Maybe you can get it reattached," Mnuchin said, while still wiping his face.

"It's too small for that," Conway said. Turning to Trump, she added: "You might not even have any scarring."

"And I wouldn't have body parts that were rejected by a rabbit reattached anyway!" he hissed. "I couldn't think of anything more humiliating." Staring at the piece of flesh on Conway's tissue, he added: "Let's just bury it."

"We'll just throw it in the trash," she replied, and helped him up. "And then we'll get you checked out by a doctor for any diseases the rabbit might have."

"I'm not going to throw a piece of history in the trash! This used to be part of the greatest President in the history of the United States – it deserves a state funeral!"

"Sir," she said anxiously, "the press will eat you alive if we hold a state funeral for a tiny piece of flesh."

"A minute ago, I was attacked by a killer rabbit, so don't lecture me on getting eaten alive," he shot back, and glowered at her as the owner of the dog emerged from those same shrubs.

"Please don't call it a killer rabbit in front of voters," she whispered, while Mnuchin approached the man and ushered him away before he could notice that the President was injured.

Having been told by his doctor that his health remained mindbogglingly excellent, Trump flew back to DC later that day. Conway and Mnuchin were sitting next to him on the Air Force One, the latter holding a small wooden box he'd procured that now contained the presidential piece of flesh, while the former was in a foul mood as she held on to a small wooden box she'd procured, which had been deemed surplus to requirements.

On Friday morning, the three of them as well as Trump's wife, FLOTUS Melania, and their ten-year-old son Barron were all dressed in black as they solemnly proceeded to the gardens at the back of the White House, Mnuchin carrying, at the boy's request, the bird cage containing the presidential parrot. Secretary of Defense Jim Mattis, generals Dunford and Milley and a dozen stern-looking soldiers were waiting for them next to a group of trees that shielded the mourners from the curious glances of tourists and reporters loitering on the other side of the black iron fence just south of Lafayette Square. Some of the servicemen had already dug a hole, and six of them now struggled to all get their hands on Mnuchin's tiny casket before lowering it into the frozen ground.

When they'd finished and retreated into the background, Trump stepped forward, bent down to pick up some soil from the small heap next to the grave and threw it on the casket, then gave a defiant thumbs-up to the other guests as they followed suit. As soon as the soldiers fired the first shot of the twenty-one-gun salute, Barron covered his ears, but the President removed his hands to ensure his son savoured the ceremony as much as he did.

When the soldiers rested their rifles on their shoulders again, Trump stepped onto the podium next to the grave. Frowning, he stared at the FLOTUS until she got the message and quickly took a tissue out of her purse and pretended to wipe away some tears. Conway instantly did likewise, while Mnuchin suddenly sobbed and covered his eyes.

"This is very, very tough for all of us," the President said. "Especially for Kellyanne and my munchkin, who were there with me when the attack happened. Many experts who I've personally known for a very, very long time have said it was the worst attack on American soil since nine eleven. And it's very hard to understand why the attack happened, especially for my wife because she doesn't speak our language. But in any case, I'd like to say a few words."

"Grab her by the pussy!" the parrot called out.

Startled, the President looked towards the bird cage. "I don't know where he got that from," he said to his audience. Turning to his pet again, he added: "I don't teach you stuff like that, do I?"

"Pussy!" it replied.

"I'm not a pussy! I wanted to fight in Vietnam – it's just that my draft number was astonishingly excellent."

"Pussy!"

"Conway, take the bird away," he said testily.

While, she picked up the cage and returned it to the Oval Office, Trump placed his hands on the sides of the podium, and smiling dreamily, he stared into the middle distance. "As I said, when I was Barron's age, this great country was involved in a brutal war where young men like him had to risk their lives to fight the Vietcong."

The colour draining from his face, Barron anxiously looked at his mother, who shook her head and mouthed: "Just ignore it."

"If I'd been there, I would have beaten the crap out of them!" he continued, and banged his fist on the podium.

"You would have sorted them out once and for all," Mnuchin said, and Conway scowled at him.

"That's right, Mnuchin, you're a great guy – the best," he replied. "They should have allowed me to fight. I might launch an investigation into why they gave me an exemption."

"I think Osama Obama was behind that," Conway said.

"You think so?" Trump asked, worried. "I'll ask the FBI to get to the bottom of that." Sighing, he added: "Anyway, getting attacked by a killer rabbit yesterday reminded me of how it must have felt to get maimed by the Vietcong, and I will not let our brave boys like Barron suffer the same kind of injuries at the hands of the North Koreans, so let's nuke them!"

Instantly, everyone started protesting, but taking the commotion as a sign of support, he smiled and added: "We'll flatten the entire country, believe me. It will be tremendous."

"Mr President, I would not recommend this course of action!" the Secretary of Defense said. "You're just going to escalate tensions in the region by going to war, especially if we drop nuclear bombs."

"You're escalating tensions between us now, Mattis," Trump hissed, glowering at him. Holding up his injured index finger, he added: "Yesterday, I had part of my body ripped off, and all you worry about is being politically correct and not offending people?"

"Mr President, you're conflating North Korea with the rabbit," General Milley said.

"And I was also thinking about China and Russia," Mattis added.

"China and Russia have nothing to do with the rabbit," Trump snapped.

"That's right," Mnuchin quickly replied, "and the generals and the Secretary of Defense fully agree with you on that. And they also believe that North Korea has nothing to do with it either. They think the situation there requires a much smarter approach than nuclear war and that you're the only person in the world who's smart enough to come up with it."

Confused yet flattered, the President looked at him. "But we mustn't forget about my finger," he said. "That would be very, very unfair. We should have a remembrance day for the attack every year."

"Of course," Mnuchin said, and everyone anxiously agreed. "But you also have to think of a smarter solution for North Korea."

While they all waited nervously for his reaction, Trump frowned and looked into the middle distance. Then he smiled at his audience and said: "I just had an idea."

The rabbit attack

In April 1979, US President Jimmy Carter was attacked by a rabbit while out fishing on his own in rural Georgia. The uncharacteristic assault happened after the animal had been chased by a pack of hound dogs. Dubbed "killer rabbit" by the press, it jumped into the water and swam towards Carter, "making strange hissing noises and gnashing its teeth" while being "intent on climbing into the Presidential boat", according to his press secretary Jody Powell. At that point, the Commander in Chief bravely "splashed some water with a paddle", prompting the bunny to turn around and swim back to the shore, Carter told CNN in 2010.

Further reading:

"Jimmy Carter explains 'rabbit attack'", CNN: http://cnn.it/2yS8XSA

"The Gospel According to Jimmy", *GQ:* http://bit.ly/2g31S9Z

The Other Side of the Story by Jody Powell

The funeral

While the thirty-ninth US President didn't have to bury any body parts after the rabbit attack, Mexico's eleven-time President Santa Anna did hold a state funeral for his amputated leg.

At home, the infamous 19th-century general is blamed for losing more than half of his country's territory to its northern neighbour through disastrous wars and land sales between 1836 and 1853. In the US, he is defined by his actions in March 1836, during the Texas Revolution. First, he ignored calls for clemency from his own generals and ordered the execution of the few survivors among the defiant, vastly outnumbered Anglo-American settlers in the mythologised Battle of the Alamo. Then he had another four hundred captured soldiers killed in what became known as the Goliad massacre.

Yet prior to these atrocities, Santa Anna had helped liberate Mexico from three centuries of Spanish rule and defeated the former colonial masters' final attempt to reconquer the country, thus becoming someone in whom his contemporaries placed "a vague confidence that he could do miracles", according to nineteenth-century writer Justo Sierra. At the same time, though, "with his constant proclamations, Santa Anna became a headache for the country," Gustavo Vazquez-Lozano writes, prompting visions of cross-border Twitter spats if the Mexican general had been around today.

Another trait Santa Anna arguably shared with Donald Trump was that he preferred gaining power to exercising it, with vice presidents left to run the country while he pursued other interests, such as organising cockfights. During his presidencies, "ceremony replaced substance", Philip Russell writes, citing as an example the understated funeral for Santa Anna's left leg.

Having lost the limb in the so-called Pastry War of 1838 – a conflict with France prompted by the Mexican government's refusal to reimburse a locally based French pastry chef whose shop had been looted – the self-styled "Napoleon of the West" initially had it buried in the grounds of his hacienda. But upon returning to power for the umpteenth time, he thought of a more suitable way to acknowledge his sacrifices for the nation. In 1842, he had the bones dug up, put in a glass case and transferred to Mexico City in a solemn parade. Accompanied by speeches, poems and cannon salvos, his leg was laid to rest at Santa Paula cemetery and a monument was built to honour it.

Santa Anna also declared the anniversary of his injury a national remembrance day. But two years later, he'd fallen out of favour again and an angry mob retrieved the bones and dragged them through the streets. Another three years after that, in 1847, Santa Anna was attacked by Illinois infantry during the Mexican-American War. He managed to escape on a horse, but the US soldiers seized his prosthetic leg, which, despite Mexico's frequent pleas to have it returned, can be seen at the Illinois State Military Museum in Springfield.

In 1876, Santa Anna died aged eighty-two, near-blind, impoverished and ignored. But in his prime he had, according to the *Encyclopædia Britannica*, "a magnetic personality and real qualities of leadership, but his lack of principles, his pride and his love of military glory and extravagance, coupled with a disregard for and incompetence in civil affairs, led Mexico into a series of disasters and himself into ill repute."

Replace Mexico with the US, and you might have the epitaph for you know who.

Further reading:

The History of Mexico: From Pre-Conquest to Present by Philip Russell

Santa Anna: The Life and Legacy of the Legendary Mexican President and General by Gustavo Vazquez-Lozano

"Illinois museum sticks to its guns over Santa Anna's leg", *Chicago Tribune:* http://trib.in/2yjlotR

An obscene parrot

At the funeral of the seventh US President, Andrew Jackson, in 1845, "a wicked parrot that was a household pet got excited and commenced swearing so loud and long as to disturb the people and had to be carried from the house", one of the mourners later recalled.

A pivotal figure in the early history of the Democrats, Jackson was "known for his bombast" yet "styled himself as a man of the people", *The New York Times* said, comparing him to Trump. Traditionally revered, Jackson has more recently been reviled because he owned slaves and signed the Indian Removal Act in 1830, a year after becoming President. This law forced Native Americans to move west so their land could be occupied by white settlers, resulting in the death of about 4,000 Cherokees during the so-called Trail of Tears. Instigated by Barack Obama's Treasury Department, Jackson's picture on the twenty-dollar bill is therefore due to be replaced with one of abolitionist Harriet Tubman in 2020.

Cue Donald Trump declaring his undying love for Jackson in what PolitiFact called "a bromance across the centuries". Perhaps remembering that, despite being a Republican President, he used to donate more money to the Democrats up until 2012, Trump installed a painting of his fellow populist in the Oval Office, visited his tomb and called him "an amazing figure in American history".

Meanwhile, Steve Bannon has repeatedly compared Trump to Jackson, though apparently not because the latter was, according to *The Atlantic,* considered "unstable and a would-be dictator", "mixed his public duties and his business" and "declared the system was rigged" when he lost the 1824 presidential elections.

Further reading:

"Jackson and Trump: How Two Populist Presidents Compare", *The New York Times*: http://nyti.ms/2n1CAO4

"What's up with Donald Trump and Andrew Jackson?", PolitiFact: http://bit.ly/2qzS9Lm

"Donald Trump and the Legacy of Andrew Jackson", *The Atlantic*: http://theatln.tc/2jDUWPJ

Andrew Jackson and Early Tennessee History Vol. 3 by Samuel Gordon Heiskell

Subordinates covered in honey

King Pepi II – who was born in 2284BC, acceded to Egypt's throne aged six and was possibly the world's longest-ruling monarch of all time, with estimates for the length of his reign ranging from sixty-four to ninety-four years – apparently had honey smeared on naked slaves, so that they became "human flypaper" and the insects would leave him alone.

Further reading:

The Unbelievable Truth, introduced by David Mitchell

Presidential offspring

Barron Trump was only ten when his father won the 2016 US elections, and upon moving to the White House a few months later, he became the first presidential son to live there since John F. Kennedy Jr in the early 1960s. Just a few months shy of sixty when Barron was born, Donald Trump was roughly the same age as the tenth US President, John Tyler, had been when he'd fathered one of his fifteen children, Lyon Gardiner. As of 2017, the latter's sons Lyon Gardiner Jr and Harrison Ruffin, born in 1924 and 1928, respectively, were still alive. This means that John Tyler – who was born in 1790, a year after George Washington became the first President of the United States – still had two surviving grandsons.

To put that in a different way: this means there is a chance that Donald Trump's grandchildren will still be around in 2173.

Further reading:

"President John Tyler Has 2 Living Grandsons", U.S. News & World Report: http://bit.ly/2mMh1lE

CHAPTER FIVE

A capital mistake

"The President will therefore no longer consider nuclear war against North Korea and pursue a different strategy instead," White House Press Secretary Sean Spicer said, as he finished his press briefing at around eleven the following Monday morning.

"Is that the reason why he flew off in his Boeing 757 last night?" a CNN reporter asked.

"He didn't fly anywhere," Spicer lied. "Air Force One is still here in Washington."

"But that appears to be a ruse because Mr Trump's personal Boeing 757 left DC last night," the reporter insisted.

"Who leaked this?"

"Nobody – when I arrived from New York this morning, I noticed that the plane wasn't at its hangar, so I asked someone who works at the airport."

"So, you didn't actually see his Boeing leave," Spicer sneered. "In other words, it's fake news. The President's private plane – which, as the word suggests, is a private matter – was probably just taken away for maintenance."

"And what about that twenty-one gun salute at the White House on Friday?" a *New York Times* journalist asked. "That was clearly an official occasion, but no one seems to know what for."

"It was just a normal gun salute," Spicer said defensively. "To suggest it was anything other than that is as ridiculous as saying there's a link between North Korea and the whereabouts of the President's private plane."

But the Press Secretary was being economical with the truth. For at precisely that moment – after a twenty-hour flight, including a sixty-minute stopover in Honolulu to refuel – the black, red and white Boeing 757 with the golden letters proclaiming TRUMP was touching down at Camp Stanley just outside Uijeongbu, South Korea. The local time was just after midnight, and under the cover of darkness, the US Commander in Chief and his two travel companions, Kellyanne Conway and Steve Mnuchin, were ushered across the frost-covered runway towards a car. They were planning to drive it to a secret destination – so secret, in fact, that not even Vincent K. Brooks, the commander of the U.S. army base located about twenty-five miles south of the North Korean border, had been told about it.

Mnuchin got behind the wheel of the black Lincoln, and as they left the army base for Pyongyang, Conway turned to the President sitting next to her in the backseat.

"It won't take us long to get to the demilitarised zone," she said.

About fifteen minutes into their journey, as one sleepy area of well-kept suburban houses gave way to another, Trump said: "This place is very quiet."

"Well, as Kellyanne said, this is the demilitarised zone," Mnuchin explained, and followed the signs towards the capital city they'd mentioned so many times before.

Half an hour later, they drove along the now mostly deserted streets of a large city with gleaming state-of-the-art skyscrapers, flashing neon signs and brand-new cars parked on the roadside.

"Where are we?" Trump asked. "This looks like a Vietcong version of New York."

"This is the capital!" Mnuchin said excitedly.

"Are you sure?" Conway asked. "We've been driving for only forty-five minutes – I thought it was meant to take at least a couple of hours."

"That's American cars for you," Trump replied. "It would take you hours in a Hyundai."

"Now we have to find Kim's palace," Mnuchin said, and slowed down as he eyed the entrances to the skyscrapers on both sides of the boulevard. "I'm not sure how, though."

"Just ask someone," Trump replied, and leaned towards the middle of the car to get a better view of the city through the windscreen. "Look, there's a McDonald's – just ask someone who works there."

"I didn't think they'd have McDonald's in North Korea," Conway said, as they parked in front of it.

"They have McDonald's everywhere – it's one of the brands that will make America great again," the President explained.

Meanwhile, Mnuchin got out of the car and braved the freezing temperatures before returning from the restaurant a minute later. Putting on his seat belt, he said: "It's just up the road, about five minutes from here."

"Did they just tell you where their dictator lives?" Conway asked, incredulous.

Starting the Lincoln again, he shrugged and said: "Yeah, they told me it's just up the road."

"That's so weird," she replied, and turned to the President.

"Well, remember this is a very secretive state, so we don't know what's going on behind the scenes," Trump cautioned. "It's probably best if we keep a low profile now that we know where that son of a bitch lives – at least until we've started putting my plan into action."

Said plan – devised in a matter of seconds during the state funeral – involved coming face to face with the armed guards at Kim Jong-un's residence. Having agreed to the strategy at the time in order to avoid nuclear war, Mnuchin now had second thoughts as he pulled up next to the road barriers in front of the driveway leading up to the palace. Turning to the President, he asked: "Are you sure you want to go ahead with this?"

"I don't see any other option," he replied, while the two soldiers patrolling the driveway eyed their car suspiciously. "Unless you prefer nuclear war."

With that, he opened the door and stepped out into the cold.

Seeing him approach, the soldiers stopped marching back and forth and instead stood and stared at him.

"Stop!" one of them barked, and both pointed their rifles at him when he got to within thirty feet.

"Put your rifles down, folks," Trump said, and raised his open hands to prove that he wasn't armed, while proceeding undeterred. "I want to speak to your dictator, Mr Kim."

Bewildered, the soldiers looked at each other and lowered their weapons as the President got closer to them. They talked in Korean for a moment, the only words Trump could understand being his own name. Then one of them said in heavily accented English: "President Kim sleepy now."

"I'm sleepy, too, folks," he replied, and smiled magnanimously. "It's been a long trip – the last time I was up for so long without sleeping was when I won the election. And by the way, I would have won the popular vote, too, if you take out the illegal votes."

Baffled, the soldiers glanced at each other. "What do you want?" the same guard asked.

"I want the illegal votes to be taken out."

The soldiers conferred in Korean. Then the one who did all the talking said: "My English is not good – I don't understand. You come here – what do you want?"

"I want to speak to the dictator because I've changed my mind – I want to become a communist."

Again, they talked in Korean. "We call President Kim now," the soldier finally said, and went inside the guard shack adorned with a white flag featuring a red and blue *Taeguk* and four black trigrams. He spoke on the phone for a couple of minutes, getting increasingly agitated while repeating the same phrase and the name Trump over and over again, as though the people on the other end of the line didn't believe him. Eventually, he hung up, then pushed buttons to open the gate and lower the road barriers before indicating for Trump to return to his car and drive onto the vast presidential premises.

"That was the easy part," Trump said, as he rejoined his aides. "Now, I have to convince Kim that I want to become a communist."

"It's amazing that you even managed to get access to him," Mnuchin said excitedly, as they slowly passed the soldiers and drove along the winding road that cut through the manicured gardens.

"There's no way Osama Obama would have managed that," the President replied. But on reflection, he added: "Actually, they'd probably just let him in because he's Muslim, too."

A minute later, they pulled up in front of Cheong Wa Dae, or Blue House, a complex of traditional Korean grey-stone buildings with blue roof tiles. As soon as the car stopped, one of the dozen or so soldiers standing in front of the imposing main building opened the door for Trump and saluted him as he got out of the Lincoln. Immediately recognising the slim fifty-odd-year-old man in a black suit who was coldly eyeing him from the top of the stairs leading to the entrance of the residence, the President went towards him, followed by Conway and Mnuchin.

"Mr President," his Korean counterpart said, looking both surprised and hostile.

"Kim, old Comrade," he replied, smiling and extending his hand, but the Korean leader skilfully avoided shaking it by using his arms to point, in an ostensibly polite way, towards the imposing, gate-like door and invite Trump in.

"Are you sure that's him?" Conway whispered, as they followed their host inside. "He looks very different from the pictures."

"It's definitely him," Trump replied. "I never forget a face."

"He's lost a lot of weight," she said.

"Well, being a dictator can be stressful," he explained, as they crossed the vast hall illuminated by a huge chandelier.

"This way," Kim said, pointing towards a door to their left.

"Your English is very good," Trump shouted, and smiled at him. Pronouncing each word individually, he loudly added: "I. Am. Very. Impressed. By. Your. English."

"Thank you," Kim said, seeming annoyed rather than thankful.

Then one of his aides opened the door and they all entered a large drawing room that was sparsely yet tastefully furnished with Oriental antiques.

"I. Like. Your. Home. Very. Much," Trump shouted, as the two of them sat down on large brown-leather wing-chairs on either side of a low glass table. "It's. Very. Exotic."

"You don't have to shout at me," Kim said testily, while Conway and Mnuchin sat down on a couple of regular chairs by the windows. "So, why have you come here?"

"Kim, old Comrade, I want to be completely honest with you, like an open book," Trump replied, speaking in a normal voice now. "By the way, have you read *The Art of the Deal*?"

Puzzled, he said uncertainly: "I don't think I know it."

"Of course, you don't – you're a communist," Trump replied, and smiled forgivingly. "It's the bible for capitalists, and all the experts in the world agree that it's the greatest book ever written. I wrote it, and I would highly recommend it. But now I want to become a communist like you because I'm terminally ill. Do you know what that means? It means I will die soon, which is very sad."

"Mr President," the Korean leader said.

"Let me finish," Trump replied. "Having this astonishingly deadly disease made me realise that there's more to life than being a rich capitalist. So, now I want to become a poor communist, too, and live in a home with barely any furniture, like you."

Frowning, Kim looked at him for a moment. "Are you serious?" he asked. "This is Seoul."

Chuckling, Trump said: "Comrade, you can say a lot about this city but not that it has soul. Believe me – we drove across this entire godforsaken place earlier on, and there was hardly anyone around. There was a McDonald's and that's about it."

"This is Seoul, the capital of *South* Korea!" Kim exclaimed.

Puzzled, Trump turned around to Conway and Mnuchin, who both got up and came over. Leaning down to the President, the Treasury Secretary whispered: "He's probably playing mind games."

"I don't think he is," Conway said, looking at her phone. "According to Google Maps, we're at the Blue House, which is the residence of the South Korean President in Seoul."

"What does that mean, Mnuchin?" Trump asked, looking up at him.

"Yes, my munchkin," Conway said gleefully, "what does that mean?"

Flustered, he looked at her, then at the President. "I guess I might have confused the names of the capital cities," he said. And more forcefully, he added: "Why do they have two capitals anyway? It doesn't make any sense!"

"That's a good point," Trump said. "I'll raise it with the South Korean President when I meet him." Turning to Kim, he asked: "So, who are you, then? I feel like I've seen you before."

"I am Kim Jung-Pyo, the President of South Korea," he replied acidly. "We met a week ago when I visited you in Washington."

"I knew it!" Trump said triumphantly. "I never forget a face. It's just names that I'm not that good with – although to be fair, it's confusing for people from the developed world because you and the North Korean Kim have the same name, but you have different capital cities, so it's hard to keep up." Smiling forgivingly, he added: "It's cultural differences."

"Cultural differences?" Kim repeated, incredulous. "And what about the cultural differences between South Korea and North Korea? How could you possibly end up in Seoul if you want to go to Pyongyang?"

"I don't know how that happened," Mnuchin said defensively. "We did cross the demilitarised zone but must have accidentally re-entered South Korea. It was very badly signposted."

"I noticed that, too," Trump said. "The road signs were in Chinese first and English only underneath, which makes it very hard to spot for the driver."

"And I didn't see any signs for the border at all," Mnuchin added adamantly. "In the United States, you wouldn't be able to just cross the border – there are lots of signs and border security."

"And soon, there'll be a border wall between America and Mexico," Trump said. "The only countries for which we won't build a wall are Canada and Europe."

Sneering, Kim shook his head. "So, why did you decide to travel to North Korea?"

"Because I've come up with a tremendous plan to defeat the other Kim once and for all," Trump replied. "I want to go to his palace and tell him that I'm about to die and that this sad news has made me think about my life and prompted me to convert to Communism, which will make him very happy. Then, while I'm staying at his palace, I'll pretend that I've died, and my munchkin and Conway will tell him that according to US law, I'll have to be buried where I died. So, they'll arrange a state funeral for me in North Korea and we'll ship over thousands of soldiers for it, and then we'll take over the country."

Sneering once again, the South Korean President turned to his aides and said something in Korean that made them laugh. Then he looked at Trump and sharply said: "Kim Jong-un is deluded and dangerous, but he's not stupid!"

"I know, that's why I've come up with this tremendous plan, because he won't be able to figure it out."

Sighing, Kim said: "Your border wall with Mexico – how much will it cost?"

"About twenty-five billion dollars. But we'll get Mexico to pay for it."

"Will they actually pay for it?" he asked sceptically.

"They have to, because Congress won't approve us paying for it."

"We'll pay for it," Kim replied. "But only if you drive back to the airport immediately and fly back home before anyone realises that you came here."

"You'll pay for it?" Trump asked, his eyebrows raised.

"Yes, because if Kim Jong-un realises that the country that is supposed to be our most important ally is run by a madman, it will compromise our national security."

"You're right, it's best to be cautious," Trump agreed. "I don't trust the Chinese President either."

"And what about our border wall with Canada?" Mnuchin asked, and winked at his baffled boss. "We'll need another twenty-five billion dollars for that."

"You've got it," Kim said, without hesitating, prompting Trump to smile at the Treasury Secretary while Conway scowled at him.

Vikings invade the wrong city

The story goes that during the Vikings' rampage across Europe, the explorer Hastein spotted a city on the western Italian coast in 860, decided it was Rome and came up with a cunning plan for an invasion. Ignoring for a moment that Rome isn't actually located by the sea, he led his Viking fleet into the harbour of what turned out to be the city of Luna. Since its fortified walls made an assault difficult, he then sent some of his men to the shore to relay the message that he, their leader, was dying and wanted to convert to Christianity at the local cathedral.

Though wary, the Lunatics welcomed the ostensibly suffering and pious Hastein, and their bishop baptised him. Afterwards, the Viking and his apparently peaceful entourage returned to their ships before one of them reappeared at the city gates at night to announce that Hastein had died. The locals granted his supposed wish to be buried in the grounds of their cathedral. But during the funeral, he jumped out of his coffin and slayed the bishop while the Viking 'mourners' killed the congregation before looting Luna and burning it to the ground when they realised the city wasn't actually Rome.

Further reading:

The Sea Wolves: A History of the Vikings by Lars Brownworth

CHAPTER SIX

An argument built on sand

When the President and his two advisers boarded his private Boeing an hour and a half later, he said: "Let's stop over in Scotland on our way back. I need to talk to the Scottish Government because they want to fine me for my golf course."

A minute later, they all sat down on the large cream leather chairs dotted around a mahogany table at the back of the plane. Both yawning, Mnuchin and Conway leaned back and looked absent-mindedly out of the windows, ready to fall asleep.

"Here we go, folks," Trump sighed. "Another very long flight." As his aides smiled sleepily at him, he said: "Let's play a game – let's think of other words for penis."

Taken aback, they were suddenly wide awake again.

Regaining his composure first, Mnuchin took advantage of Conway's hesitancy and said: "Sure, why not?"

"Really?" she asked, frowning at him as though he'd made the suggestion. "It seems a bit childish to me."

"Don't be a pussy," Trump said. "What are we going to do otherwise for the next twelve hours?"

"I really don't want to play that game," she replied, looking uncomfortable. "It seems inappropriate."

"It's just a game," Mnuchin said, earning himself an angry look.

"Exactly," Trump agreed. "Come on, you start, Kellyanne."

Sighing, she said: "OK – manhood."

"Blue-vein sausage," Mnuchin said, and looked at Trump.

"Fuck rod."

Conway grimaced.

"Come on, your turn," the President said impatiently.

Reluctantly, she said: "Best friend."

"Beaver basher," Mnuchin said.

"Flesh flute."

"I really don't want to play this game any more," Conway begged. "It's not very presidential."

"Oh, come on, don't be a pussy," Mnuchin said.

"Here's a good one," Trump said. "Custard launcher."

But without another word, she got up and went to the front part of the plane, while the President and Mnuchin chuckled and the latter gleefully said: "Purple-headed yogurt flinger."

"Ha, that's a good one," Trump said, laughing. "You're a great guy, Mnuchin – the best!"

Having arrived at Aberdeen Airport at about three o'clock on a crisp yet sunny February afternoon, the President and his two advisers were picked up by an employee of Trump International Golf Links. Escorted by a police motorcade on this less secretive leg of their round-the-world trip, they were driven to nearby nineteenth-century stone mansion MacLeod House & Lodge, which, although described as "tremendous" and "the best" in the marketing brochure, was almost empty at this time of year. After they'd freshened up, Trump took his aides to his adjacent golf course to illustrate the contentious issue raised by the Scottish Government.

"Wow, this place is beautiful," Conway gushed, as they walked across one of the greens, away from the setting sun and towards the North Sea shore, with three dozen policemen patrolling the fairways but keeping their distance. "I love the dunes."

"Do they look like dunes to you?" Trump asked, frowning at her as they approached them.

"Yes, they're beautiful," she said.

"Mnuchin?"

"They're beautiful," he agreed.

"But are they dunes?"

Seeing the frown on Trump's face, he hesitated. "I'm not sure."

"I'm not sure either," the President said. "To me, it looks like sand that's been blown into different shapes by the wind."

"Isn't that the definition of dunes?" Conway asked.

"Are you some kind of sandologist now?" Mnuchin sneered, and received an angry look.

"There must be some other name for it," Trump said, prodding the sand with his shoe. "The Scottish Government says these are dunes that need to be protected, and they claim we've destroyed them. They keep sending people here to assess the damage, and now they want me to pay a huge fine, which is very, very unfair. So, I need to prove to them that these aren't dunes."

"They clearly aren't dunes," Mnuchin said. "It's just sand."

"That's what I think," Trump agreed. "Let's get a sandologist to prove it."

"There's no such thing as a sandologist," Conway replied.

"Yes, there is. Am I right, Mnuchin?"

"Of course, you're right," he said, prompting another scowl.

"I trust Mnuchin," Trump said to her. Then he looked at him and added: "I want you to find one – we're going to Edinburgh first thing tomorrow morning to present our case to the Scottish Government, and we need the sandologist to give evidence."

Panicking, Mnuchin looked at Conway, who was delighted. "That's very short notice," he replied. "Where am I going to find a sandologist so quickly?"

"Well, at least you know more about sandology than I do, right?" she said gleefully. "Don't let the President down, my munchkin."

"Yes, don't let me down – I'm relying on you."

Instantly, the Treasury Secretary took his phone out of his coat pocket, and heading off across the dunes while the President and Conway walked back towards the fairways, he anxiously googled oil companies in nearby Aberdeen, the oil capital of Europe, figuring they'd employ geologists.

Which indeed they did. However, upon hearing that he wanted them to testify on behalf of Donald Trump, each of them immediately declined, saying they didn't want to risk their careers by being associated with the President.

Watching Conway talk animatedly to Trump as they wandered off into the sunset and towards the club house, Mnuchin saw his career crumbling before his eyes. Unable to bear the sight of her ingratiating herself, he turned around and wistfully looked towards the grey North Sea when he spotted a man sitting on a dune who was picking up sand and examining it. Hoping that evicting a hostile Scottish Government agent would soften the blow of not finding a sandologist, he stomped towards him, though on closer inspection he realised it was just an elderly rambler.

"Good afternoon," the grey-bearded, silver-haired man said in a thick Scottish accent, and smiled at Mnuchin. "It's been a lovely day today, hasn't it?"

"Yes, it has," he sighed, and looked towards the sea.

"Are you American?"

"Yes."

"But you don't work for Donald Trump, do you?"

"I do," he said warily.

"You do?" the man replied excitedly. "He's not here at the moment, though, is he?"

"We arrived an hour ago."

"Really? So, are you a secret service agent?"

"No, I …" Mnuchin said, tailing off as he scrutinised the man's face. But given that he seemed harmless, he admitted: "I'm the Treasury Secretary of the United States."

"Holy mackerel!" he exclaimed. "Are you serious?"

"Yes."

"So, what are you doing here in winter? Doesn't Trump have another golf course in Florida?"

"We're here because of the dunes."

"Of course, the dunes," he said, rolling his eyes. "People round here like to get their knickers in a twist over a bit of sand."

"I saw you picking up some and looking at it," Mnuchin said, as he tried to figure out what to make of the man.

"Well, I used to work as a geologist for some of the oil firms in the area, so examining stone fragments is my professional habit."

Nodding towards the ground the man was sitting on, the Treasury Secretary asked: "And do you think these are dunes?"

Surprised, he said: "What else would they be?"

"I don't know," Mnuchin replied uncertainly. "I was hoping you might have an alternative definition. Mr Trump wants to go to the Scottish Government tomorrow and argue that these aren't dunes."

"Oh, right," he said, and picked up some sand again. Examining it closely, he added: "Well, you could argue that, technically, some of these stone fragments are gravel rather than sand. And if most of it was gravel, then they wouldn't be dunes because dunes, by definition, are made up of sand. But you'd have to deal with some pretty daft people for them to believe that this is mostly gravel. So, you're lucky that you're dealing with the Scottish Government."

His heart racing, the Treasury Secretary asked: "What's the difference between sand and gravel?"

After the man had explained the difference, Mnuchin took a deep breath. "Sir," he said, "would you be willing to come to the Scottish Government with us tomorrow morning and testify that this landscape is made up of gravel rather than sand? I know that Mr Trump is not universally admired, but before you object, let me tell you that he is –"

"Very rich," the man butted in, and smiled mischievously. "So, it depends on how much is in it for me."

Looking as though he was about to burst with joy, Mnuchin said: "Sir, I ..." Then he abruptly leaned down and hugged him. "Thank you so much!" he added, beaming while the man chuckled. "What's your name, by the way?"

"Andrew Mac a' Mhuilleir."

"Andrew Mac-mm-mm-ley," he repeated. "And you'll really testify for us? Because all the geologists I've spoken to didn't want to have anything to do with the President because they thought it would harm their job prospects if they did."

"Yeah, but I'm retired," he said, smiling. "I'm not looking for work, so I don't care what people think. What I care about is how much money Donald Trump is willing to pay to top up my pension."

"Great," Mnuchin said. "Then let's go and meet him."

Having picked up some samples to support their argument, they went to the heavily guarded club house and found Trump and Conway sitting at one of the walnut tables inside The Dunes restaurant, heads close to each other as he said: "I trust you more than anybody else."

"This is Andrew Mac-mm-mm-ley," Mnuchin said, interrupting them, and they both looked at him and his companion. "He's a retired geologist." Seeing Conway's look of surprise turn to horror, the Treasury Secretary gleefully added: "He will testify for us."

The following morning at seven o'clock, all four of them boarded a helicopter for the forty-five-minute flight to the Scottish Parliament in Edinburgh. Arriving at the sprawling, abstract modernist building that was supposed to look like it had grown out of the landscape, Trump led his entourage to the debating chamber, where they walked into a parliamentary session.

Dumbfounded, the MPs stared at the President breezing in, followed by his lackeys, and heading straight for the podium at the front. Turning around when he reached it, Trump took in his audience sitting at sycamore desks arranged in a horseshoe-shaped layout. "Wow, what a turnout!" he said, and smiled. Looking at his team, he added: "Isn't that amazing?"

"It's incredible," Mnuchin said, receiving a puzzled look from Mac a' Mhuilleir and an angry one from Conway. "It's the biggest turnout for a US President ever."

"That's incredible," Trump said. Addressing the MPs, he added: "So, let's get started straight away, folks – we're here to discuss my golf course."

"Maybe you are, but we're not discussing that right now," Alex Salmond, the former First Minister of Scotland, replied angrily, and rose from his seat in the semi-circle to join his one-time friend and current foe at the podium.

Having initially supported Trump's plans for the golf course on the basis that it was supposed to be "the best" and create a "tremendous" number of jobs, he'd vigorously complained once it had transpired that the main effect of the project was the damage it caused – despite repeated promises to the contrary – to the area's environmentally protected dunes.

"We are busy discussing our need for Scottish independence, so we really don't have any time for this right now," he added, and stood next to the President.

"Do you guys ever talk about anything else?" Trump asked sarcastically. "Is that why the UK paid for this building, so you can come here and talk about how amazing it would be to be independent from them even though it'll never happen?"

Everyone booed, while Salmond seemed flustered yet insisted: "We discuss other things, as well."

"Like what?"

"Like policies."

"What policies?"

"Well, we ... we ... we want to make Scotland great again."

"That'll never happen," Trump replied. "This country would be totally irrelevant without the UK."

As the MPs booed again, he put his hand on Mac a' Mhuilleir's shoulder and added: "But you do have some tremendous people here in Scotland, like this man, Andrew Mac-mm-mm-ley, who is very, very famous because he's the greatest sandologist in the world. And he wants to tell you something."

Extending his left arm to invite the geologist onto the podium where the Presiding Officer and his two deputies were sitting, he said as the debating chamber calmed down again: "Andrew, take a seat."

Alarmed at the prospect of Donald Trump taking over her parliament, Scottish First Minister Nicola Sturgeon rose from her seat in the front row of the semi-circle and called out: "Mr President!"

Turning around as he ushered Mac a' Mhuilleir up the steps, Trump smiled half-heartedly, waved and said: "Hi there, very nice to meet you."

Then he followed the geologist, indicated for the Presiding Officer and his deputies to leave and sat down on the executive chair in the centre, while Mac a' Mhuilleir took the smaller seat to his right.

As Salmond and Sturgeon looked on impotently, Trump turned to his expert and said: "Please go ahead, Professor."

Holding on to the hundred-thousand-dollar cheque in his trouser pocket, the geologist said: "Good morning everyone. My name is Andrew Mac a' Mhuilleir, and I'm a retired geologist with an undergraduate degree from the University of Aberdeen, where I spent forty years working for various oil companies. Having forensically examined the mounds next to Mr Trump's golf course near Balmedie, I have found evidence that parts of them consist of gravel rather than sand. This means those mounds cannot possibly be dunes, as the Scottish Government claims, because dunes are, by definition, composed of accumulated grains of sand, not gravel."

Sneering, Salmond looked at his fellow MPs. Then he turned to Mac a' Mhuilleir again and asked: "What's the difference between sand and gravel?"

"According to the Udden-Wentworth scale, which is used to classify different types of sediment, sand is defined as particles with a diameter of between 0.0625 and two millimetres, and gravel as particles with a diameter of between two and 4.096 millimetres," he explained, and took a small transparent plastic bag out of his pocket. Taking out one of the three tiny rock fragments inside and holding it up, he added: "These are random samples I retrieved from Trump International Golf Links, all of which are exactly two millimetres long, so they could be defined as gravel."

"But they could also be defined as sand, based on what you just said," Salmond pointed out.

"That's correct – it's open to interpretation. Which means it's also open to interpretation whether the mounds at Trump International Golf Links are dunes or not."

"That means I haven't damaged any dunes because there aren't any," Trump said.

"Based on the three grains of sand you've hand-picked to support your theory," Salmond scoffed. "Though presumably the rest of them are smaller than two millimetres because otherwise you would have just scooped up a handful and put them in your bag rather than carefully selecting them."

"You can't just say that without having any evidence for it because that would be very, very unfair," Trump replied. "We've given you the evidence here in court, and since you don't have any evidence to contradict Professor Mac-mm-mm-ley you have to close the case immediately because this isn't some medieval English court where you don't have to produce any evidence."

"Well, first of all this isn't England; second of all this isn't a court; and thirdly, we don't keep samples of the sand from your golf course at the Scottish Parliament," Salmond said testily. "Plus, we commissioned several studies that proved beyond any reasonable doubt that the dunes at Trump International Golf Links are thousands of years old and that despite your repeated promises to ensure that this unique national treasure would remain intact, they have started to disintegrate because of the work you have undertaken."

"Those people you sent to do the studies were not qualified sandologists and they have treated me very, very unfairly," Trump replied. "Andrew is the best sandologist in the world, and he just told you that it's science, so you can't argue with that because he's a great guy."

"It's absolute bloody nonsense to say they aren't dunes!" Salmond hissed. "They are made up of sand, and they look exactly like dunes. And you know that as well as I do. I mean, come on – even the restaurant at Trump International Golf Links is called The Dunes."

"Yes, but we're renaming it. We found out only recently that my golf course isn't surrounded by dunes but by gravel, so now we're renaming it The Gravel. That was an honest mistake, so you can't punish me for that because that would be very,

very unfair. People make mistakes, and you know that better than most people."

"The only mistake I've made is to allow you to build that bloody golf course," he snapped.

"You've made plenty of other mistakes, believe me," the President said. "The FBI and the CIA have shown me some tremendous evidence, but I'm not allowed to talk about it here. And by the way, I think you're cheating on your wife. I know you are."

Instantly, the chamber exploded with noise, everybody shouting and MPs getting up and furiously pointing at Trump.

"Where's Maggie?" he said, scanning his chaotic audience.

"Who is Maggie?" Salmond asked, angry and perplexed.

"Your boss, the English President. She promised me to sort this out."

"Her name is Theresa, and she's in London," he said testily, and shook his head as he turned to Sturgeon.

"I'll call her," Trump replied, and took his phone out of his pocket. "She has to come here and sort this out."

"Well, she can't because this is a matter for the Scottish Government. Plus, right now, she's busy dealing with the fallout from the riots the other week anyway."

When the British Prime Minister arrived two hours later, Trump and his advisers returned from their break, and sitting down on his Presiding Officer chair, he summoned her to the podium.

"These people here treat me very, very unfairly, and you promised to sort it out," he said angrily.

"I'm terribly sorry," she replied, wringing her hands. "I've just been rather busy dealing with the fallout from the riots."

"Well, you just have to sign it off now – we've already provided some tremendous evidence to prove that I'm right," he said, then took his phone out and tweeted: "Very sad to hear about the riots in the UK. The country needs a stronger leader!"

"Hold on, not so fast," Salmond said, and stepped up to the podium. "That so-called evidence rests on the flimsiest of premises," he added, and explained the difference between sand and gravel to the Prime Minister.

"Well, it does seem to be open to interpretation," she said uncertainly, and looked at Trump for approval.

"With all due respect, Prime Minister," Salmond said, "the President and his so-called sandologist have produced three grains of sand – or gravel, as they like to call it – as supporting evidence. By contrast, we have carried out several environmental impact assessments that have all highlighted how much damage the work commissioned by Mr Trump has caused to this very fragile ecosystem that has been described as Scotland's Amazon."

"Scotland has nothing like that brand," Trump said. "And those piles of gravel aren't dunes."

"Of course, they're dunes!" Salmond exclaimed, and took his phone out of his pocket to show May online pictures of them. "It's absolute bloody nonsense to say they aren't. Here, Prime Minister, have a look yourself."

Examining the images, she hesitated. "Well, I'm not a sandologist," she said apologetically, and smiled at Trump.

"Oh, come on," Salmond called out, and put his phone away again.

"Maggie, you need to deal with this man," Trump said sternly. "He treats me very, very unfairly."

"Why do you let him call you Maggie?" Salmond asked, exasperated.

Chuckling nervously, May shrugged. "I don't mind it," she said, smiling. "I take it as a compliment because it suggests that he sees me as a strong leader."

"I need you to sort this out," Trump reminded her.

"Couldn't we just turn a blind eye?" she begged Salmond. "He is the American President after all."

"Prime Minister, with all due respect, this is a Scottish issue, not a British one, and we will do whatever is right for our country."

"But remember, it's my property," Trump replied.

Scowling at him, Salmond said: "It's public land that was sold to you on condition that you'd create a tremendous number of jobs, which you haven't done, and that you wouldn't damage our precious, environmentally protected dunes, which you have done. So, if you refuse to pay the fine and to protect the dunes, we will simply take back the land."

"OK, I'll protect the dunes," he replied, got up and led his entourage out to the helicopter without saying another word.

Moments after takeoff, he called the Chairman of the Joint Chiefs of Staff, Joe Dunford. "What's our military capacity in the UK?" he asked, as they flew over Edinburgh on their way back to Trump International Golf Links.

"We've got about ten Air Force bases there," the general replied. "Plus, the *USS Philippine Sea* and the *USS George H W Bush* are currently in Portsmouth for a joint training exercise with Royal Navy aircraft carriers."

"I want you to pull them out of that training exercise and send them to Aberdeen immediately, so they can protect my golf course."

"Sir, you can't do that," Dunford said, taken aback. "You can't use the United States Navy to protect your private property."

But looking at the Firth of Forth estuary below as they flew north, Trump imagined he was flying over the Mekong Delta in an open-door military helicopter in around 1969 and said: "I am the Commander in Chief of our Armed Forces, and this is an order."

Twenty-four hours later, on Thursday, the two aircraft carriers arrived in Scotland and anchored in front of "the best" golf course. At the same time, reporters from around the world lined the shore and forgot all about the solar eclipse due to occur the next day, which had offered rare exciting news during two weeks dominated by talk of impending apocalyptic war and lost nuclear bombs.

Having denounced Alex Salmond on Twitter as "an embarrassment to Scotland" while refusing to speak to him or Theresa May, Trump finally relented after a day of playing golf and agreed to meet them aboard the *USS Philippine Sea* on the morning of the eclipse.

"Mr President, we can't continue like this," Salmond said, while May nodded anxiously. "Look," he added amicably, "we're here to find a solution."

"Maybe you are, but I'm not discussing that right now," Trump said, and practised his signature.

"You invited us," Salmond hissed, but immediately composed himself again. Calmly, he added: "We need to resolve this stalemate somehow."

"OK, I'll request more aircraft carriers," Trump said nonchalantly, as the commanding officer of the ship, Captain Peter Nilsen, entered the meeting room to let them know that the moon was about to drift across the face of the sun.

Having gone to the deck, Salmond and May put on their protective goggles while Trump used his hand to shield his eyes from the glaring light. And as vastly greater powers suddenly created an eerie darkness, the three politicians smiled at each other, and taking the lead, May said: "How about we put the fine on hold for now, and then we'll revisit the issue after the end of Mr Trump's presidency?"

Briefly hesitating, Salmond looked at the President, shrugged and said: "That sounds like an acceptable compromise to me."

"OK, let's call it a draw for now," Trump replied. And shaking hands with Salmond, he didn't push and pull him all over the place for once.

Leonardo da Vinci's synonyms for penis

The quintessential Renaissance Man, Leonardo da Vinci, had a profound knowledge of many things, including synonyms for penis.

As well as creating the world's most famous painting, the Mona Lisa, and dreaming up designs for future inventions such as parachutes, helicopters and diving equipment, the Tuscan polymath born in 1452 produced drawings that showed the human physique in such astonishing detail that a British surgeon used Leonardo's depictions of the human heart in 2005 to pioneer a way to repair valve damage.

Fittingly for someone so familiar with the human body, Leonardo knew many different words for *cazzo*, the Italian for "cock". And perhaps to let off steam after describing an early concept for a steam engine, he scribbled them down on folio forty-four of his *Codex Arundel*, a collection of drawings, diagrams and notes on science, art and personal matters that is now owned by London's British Library.

Further reading:

Codex Arundel, Leonardo da Vinci: http://bit.ly/1JJTqDt

Leonardo da Vinci: Experience, Experiment and Design by Martin Kemp

Ambiguous definitions

When a dispute arose in 1961 because French fishermen were catching spiny lobsters a hundred miles off Brazil's coast, both nations decided that the only sensible solution was to get their navies on the case.

While France argued that the crustaceans swim, Brazil maintained that they crawl across the seafloor, as a 1958 Geneva convention gave countries exclusive rights to all organisms that were in "constant physical contact" with their continental shelf. Wasting no time with diplomacy, the South Americans sent in warships to demand that the French boats retreat. Outraged given that exclusive fishing rights extended only a few miles from the shore at the time, the intruding fishermen refused and asked their government to send a destroyer to defuse – or in any case resolve – the situation.

In response, Brazil's military mobilised a Boeing B-17 Flying Fortress, while Foreign Minister Hermes Lima declared: "The attitude of France is inadmissible, and our government will not retreat. The lobster will not be caught."

Yet, the French didn't budge, and during a three-year standoff, both countries considered warfare to settle whether spiny lobsters swim or not. Eventually, they struck a financial deal, but Brazil also unilaterally extended its territorial waters to within two hundred nautical miles from the shore. This became the international standard in 1982 as part of the UN Convention on the Law of the Sea.

More importantly, in 1966, a wholly unbiased tribunal in northern France ruled that French fishermen caught the crustaceans in those moments when they didn't touch the seafloor, which meant they were essentially fish at that time.

This prompted Brazilian Navy Admiral and oceanography expert Paulo Moreira da Silva to remark that his country would accept that rationale as long as the French agreed with the Brazilians that a kangaroo is a bird when it hops.

Further reading:

"Brazil: Force de Flap", *Time:* http://ti.me/2fDx52Q

War, Peace and International Politics by David Ziegler

The Eclipse of Thales

While doubts persist regarding the frequently made claim that Greek philosopher Thales of Miletus was the first person in history to accurately predict a solar eclipse, the one named after him because of his supposed feat allegedly had consequences on the battlefield that he most certainly didn't anticipate.

The Medes of what is now north-western Iran and the Lydians of present-day western Turkey had been at war for five years, with both kingdoms evenly matched, when the moon passed directly across the face of the sun during their clashes on 28 May 585BC. Thales may or may not have expected this stellar event, the main supporting evidence being an account by Greek historian Herodotus, who was born about a hundred years later. In any case, the same writer also claimed that the two armies were surprised by the eclipse, and petrified, they instantly stopped fighting, with King Alyattes of Lydia and King Cyaxares of Media "anxious to have terms of peace agreed on" and calling it a draw.

Further reading:

The History of Herodotus by Herodotus: http://bit.ly/2xLCD6e

CHAPTER SEVEN
Promising the moon

Having played a round of golf on Friday afternoon after the eclipse, Donald Trump, along with his two aides, boarded his private plane on Saturday morning to return to Washington. The weather in the capital was milder now, and back at the White House, he gleefully watched for a moment as the foundations for the Trump Monument were laid on the South Lawn. But as soon as he reached the Oval Office, bad news caught up with him once more.

"Sir, there are violent protests in Charlottesville over the removal of a statue of Confederate General Robert E. Lee," White House Press Secretary Sean Spicer informed him. "And the media have found out that the North Korean soldiers and the wire mesh General Vincent K. Brooks showed them were fake."

"I hate the media," Trump grumbled, as he sat down in his executive chair and fired up his computer. "They're so dishonest."

"Well, at least Charlottesville will take the focus off the wire mesh," Spicer sighed. "And once you've put out a statement about the protests, that will distract the media even more."

"OK, I'll tweet that Lee was a tremendous guy who must not be forgotten because he tried to do so much for the white people in our country."

"Please don't write that," Spicer pleaded, and stepped towards the President's desk. "Just say something like 'I condemn the violence' – otherwise, please don't say anything at all."

"Condemn the violence," he sneered. "What's next? Do we stop celebrating the second of July?"

"Fourth of July."

"Or do we repaint Uncle Sam with a black face?"

"Just don't say anything that includes the words 'black' or 'white'," Spicer begged.

"I won't say anything at all, then," he sulkily replied.

"I think that's probably best. Let's just wait it out – eventually, it'll blow over."

"Hum," Trump said, frowning at him.

"What about the Trump Monument, though?" Spicer asked.

Turning around in his chair to look at the construction work taking place outside the Georgian windows, he smiled and said: "It seems to be coming along really well."

"Shouldn't we tear it down now that the press have found out that we didn't actually cross into North Korea?"

"We're not tearing down that statue!" Trump said angrily, and turned back towards the Press Secretary. "Tearing down statues that are part of the history of our country is morally wrong." Then he logged on to Twitter and posted that same message with several exclamation marks.

Afterwards, he scrutinised his aide's face for a moment. "Spicer," he said eventually, "can I ask you a question?"

"Of course, Sir."

"Which side are you on?"

Blushing, the Press Secretary asked: "How do you mean, Sir?"

"Why do you want to tear down the Trump Monument?"

"That's just a misunderstanding," he said anxiously. "I love the monument – I was just wondering if it's still appropriate."

"I think you better leave now," Trump said icily, and rang Reince Priebus while Spicer left the Oval Office. "Reince, I want you to hire more construction workers so the Trump Monument will be finished as quickly as possible," he instructed the White House Chief of Staff.

Then he rose from his leather chair and stood by the windows to look at the construction site again. Suddenly, he had an idea, and picking up the phone on his desk once more, he redialled Priebus's number and said: "I need a painter, as well."

A couple of hours later, he was explaining his concept to a middle-aged painter when Spicer returned to the Oval Office and announced: "A civil-rights activist was killed by a white supremacist in Charlottesville!"

"Not now," Trump replied. "I'm busy."

"Sir, you need to respond to this," the Press Secretary said adamantly.

Eyeing him suspiciously, he said: "Earlier on, you told me that I shouldn't say anything at all, but now you all of a sudden want me to respond – how come?"

"Mr President," Spicer pleaded, and looked nervously at him.

"I'm busy," he repeated. "I think you better leave now."

As Trump's Twitter account remained unusually quiet over the next forty-eight hours, the pressure on him to acknowledge the murder of a peaceful protester gradually increased along with the volume of calls for him to resign.

Having watched TV all day on Sunday, the President did the same on Monday, and noticing the growing clamour for his head, he summoned Sean Spicer to the Oval Office that afternoon.

"You're fired!" he said, and pointed at the door.

"What for?" Spicer asked, flabbergasted.

"You told me not to say anything about the protests in Charlottesville, so that's what I did. But now the fake media says that since I haven't said anything, I should resign, which is very, very unfair."

"I did advise you to respond – I just asked you not to say that Lee must not be forgotten because he tried to do so much for white people."

"If you're denying that General Lee tried to do a lot for white people, you're just as dishonest as the fake press. So, clearly, I can't trust you any more than I can trust *The New York Times*. Now leave me alone."

As Spicer trotted off, the President stared at the large TV on the wall, where yet another report featured politicians, academics and members of the public calling for his head. After watching for a while, he sighed, picked up the phone on his desk and called his most trusted adviser.

"I need my munchkin," he softly said into the receiver.

Flattered and surprised, Conway said: "Mr President, what can I do for you?"

"Is that you, Mnuchin?" he asked, and looked at the receiver.

"It's Kellyanne Conway," she said acidly.

"Oh, right. Well, I want you to come to the White House, too – I need your advice."

Instantly, she pulled herself together and said: "I'm on my way."

Twenty minutes later, both presidential advisers arrived at the same time and tried to squeeze past each other to enter the Oval Office before the other one did.

"Finally," Trump sighed, as they scrambled towards his desk and sat down on the two chairs opposite him. "Where have you been? The media have been insulting me all day!"

"I'm very sorry, Mr President," Conway replied.

"I'm even sorrier," Mnuchin said, earning him an angry look.

To gain the upper hand, she quickly added: "But you can still salvage the situation by listening to my advice. All you have to do is to publicly acknowledge the events in Charlottesville."

Surprised, Trump looked at her. "You really think if I do that, the media will apologise to me?"

"I don't know about that," she said uncertainly. "But it'll help your approval ratings if you say that the stuff that happened there is terrible."

"Well, it is terrible," he replied. "General Lee was a great man – they shouldn't have removed his statue!"

"I meant the violence."

"Oh, come on," Trump sneered. "He fought in the Civil War, so of course there was violence."

"Exactly," Mnuchin said, and the President gave him an approving look.

Annoyed, Conway said: "They removed his statue because he thought white people were superior to black people."

"You make it sound like he endorsed the Ku Klux Klan, which he didn't," Mnuchin said.

"But he didn't speak out against them either," she said.

"That doesn't mean he was a racist."

"To call Lee a racist would be a horrible accusation," Trump agreed. "Very, very nasty and unfair." Turning to his computer, he started typing as he added: "So, the civil-rights activist who got killed only had herself to blame because it was very, very nasty and unfair of her to protest against such a lovely man."

"Please don't tweet that," Conway said, alarmed. As he frowned at her while his hands hovered over the keyboard, she added: "I'd suggest you visit Charlottesville instead, say how terrible the last few days have been and how sad you are about that, etcetera, etcetera, and at the same time, you announce some big news that completely overshadows everything to distract the media from the fact that you took so long to respond to the violence."

Looking at Mnuchin, Trump asked: "Do you think that's what I should do?"

Hesitating as he looked at Conway, the Treasury Secretary reluctantly said: "I guess so."

"Hum," the President said pensively, and leaned back in his leather chair. Then his face lit up and he added: "Actually, I do have some big news!"

Within minutes, he and his two advisers were sitting in the state limousine and on their way to Maryland's Joint Base Andrews, home of the Air Force One. Taking on Sean Spicer's old role, Conway informed the media that Trump was going to give a speech at the recently renamed Emancipation Park – formerly Lee Park – in the centre of Charlottesville. Hundreds of reporters were therefore already fighting for the best positions when her boss took to the presidential podium an hour and a half later.

As darkness fell and a full moon rose over the picturesque Virginian city, the huge audience swiftly segregated into one half that booed the President and another that cheered him. Looking at the thousands of people who'd turned up, Trump smiled contently. Then he put his game face on.

"The last few days have been terrible," he said solemnly, and everyone – whether peacefully promoting civil rights or carrying the torch and other weapons for white supremacy – agreed. "The fake media have been very nasty to me, which has made me very, very sad," he continued, and the white supremacists booed the assembled journalists for making the President sad. "And they have been nasty to the innocent people who admire Robert E. Lee, who, by the way, was a tremendous guy and very,

very open-minded because he never endorsed or spoke out against the Ku Klux Klan, so he was very, very open-minded about them."

Now, the civil-rights activists shouted in anger, and to keep the peace, he added like a good parent: "Yes, I know, both sides are to blame. And yes, somebody died, etcetera, etcetera. But above all, those sons of bitches who came here to disrupt the peaceful protest in memory of Robert E. Lee have to calm down!"

Instantly, the white supremacists raised their rifles and furiously told the civil-rights nuts to calm down.

Meanwhile, Trump stared into the middle distance and muttered dreamily: "Such a lovely guy, folks. Such a lovely guy." Observing the raging crowd as people pointed and shouted abuse at each other, he said: "The dishonest media are creating divisions in our country, and we cannot allow them to do that. It's their fault that someone died here in Charlottesville because they told some very bad people that some very good people were holding a very peaceful protest here to remember General Lee. Because, folks, seriously, how can a peaceful protest lead to violence unless another group turns up to disrupt the peaceful protest?"

While his supporters brandished their guns again, he asked: "And by the way, have I told you that we will protect the Second Amendment?" As the biggest cheers of the night drowned out the civil-rights protesters, he added: "We will do it, believe me. And by the way, have I told you that I love this city? Isn't this a wonderful city? Such a peaceful city. Just look at the full moon, folks – isn't it peaceful? I think this is a tremendous city, even though we didn't win Virginia in the elections."

As his supporters booed, he said: "Yes, we didn't win here. But, boy, did we win the elections! And I promise you, folks, next time, we'll win Virginia, too, and then we'll put Robert E. Lee's statue back up!"

While his supporters roared deliriously, Conway tapped his shoulder to remind him not to say anything controversial and instead reveal the big news to distract the press.

"Oh, yes, folks, I want to show you something," he said, and beckoned her and Mnuchin to hold up his large, square surprise next to the podium.

Once they stood in front of the audience, he pulled off the sheet that covered the surprise and revealed a painting of himself as Uncle Sam.

"How about that, folks?" he asked, smiling broadly.

As his voters erupted in thunderous cheers, he revelled in their admiration and looked at the brilliant moon, then added: "How about that for a message to North Korea not to mess with us? And to show them that we're serious, I'm going to ask Nasa and our military to nuke the moon and blow up the goddamn thing! Kim thinks he's got nuclear bombs? We'll show him nuclear bombs! It's going to be tremendous, believe me – we'll get the highest TV ratings ever."

Over the moon, the white supremacists raised their weapons in the air upon hearing the good news and shouted: "Lock her up! Lock her up!" Then the President left the podium, high-fiving his supporters on the way to his limousine, while Conway and Mnuchin carried the painting as they followed him.

When he was about to get into the car, a white middle-aged lady wearing a "Blacks for Trump" T-shirt and holding a puppy in her arms called out: "Mr President!" His left hand already on the car door, he turned towards her as she added: "I want to give you this dog as a present."

"Thank you, but —"

"Take it!" Conway whispered.

"I don't like dogs," he replied.

"But the voters like their President to have a dog, which is why most Presidents have one. You can always give it to Barron."

He considered this for a moment, then said: "OK, but I don't want to touch it, so you go and get it."

As Conway went towards the lady, Trump smiled at the latter, gave her a thumbs-up and said: "We'll call him Protesto."

A dog called Looty

While cities across the UK boast monuments and streets that honour slave traders (with the one named after James Penny in Liverpool posing a conundrum for renaming campaigns since Penny Lane is now mainly associated with the Beatles song), Queen Victoria found a different way to make light of brutality.

Having effectively colonised parts of China in the nineteenth century, Britain swamped the country with opium to make money. The British government was therefore aghast when the Chinese introduced measures to prevent their citizens from getting addicted to the drug, so it launched two so-called Opium Wars. The second of these lasted from 1856 to 1860, when the victorious British and their French allies sent several envoys with a no-nonsense peace treaty to the Chinese Emperor at what is now called the Old Summer Palace outside Beijing.

Understandably already on edge, the Chinese took offence to a perceived slight and imprisoned the delegation before torturing all and killing some of them. In response, British and French soldiers looted the palace, seizing a rumoured one and a half million items before Britain's High Commissioner to China, Lord Elgin, delivered the coup de grâce by ordering his troops to burn the entire structure to the ground in what he described as a "solemn act of retribution".

Today, few people in the UK are aware of this atrocity, but in China, it echoes through the ages, still inspiring movies, debates and anger about international art sales. At the time, French writer Victor Hugo furiously denounced his country and Britain as "two robbers breaking into a museum, devastating, looting and burning, leaving laughing hand-in-hand." And Queen Victoria clearly must have had a little giggle when she received one of the looted Pekingese dogs as a present since she named it Looty. The royal family's official website nonchalantly avoids the history associated with the pooch, focusing instead on the fact that it was considered "a most affectionate and intelligent little creature" and that it became "quite the celebrity".

Further reading:

"A History of Royal Dogs", official website of the British royal family: https://www.royal.uk/history-royal-dogs?page=3

"Looty", Royal Collection Trust: http://bit.ly/2fGcLxZ

Nuking the moon

When things were heating up during the Cold War, both sides were keen to prove their strength to their enemy – and what better way to do that than to blow up the moon?

That was precisely the thinking in the US military in 1958, when physicist Dr Leonard Reiffel was tasked with what he later deemed "a PR exercise".

"The theory was that if the bomb exploded on the edge of the moon, the mushroom cloud would be illuminated by the sun," he told *The Observer* in May 2000. "The explosion would obviously be best on the dark side of the moon," he said, adding that the project euphemistically entitled "A Study of Lunar Research Flights" was "certainly technically feasible".

Ultimately, however, Dr Reiffel was glad that the "giant leap for mankind" Neil Armstrong talked about in 1969, when he became the first person to walk on the moon, wasn't a reference to us blowing up the goddamn thing.

Further reading:

"US planned one big nuclear blast for mankind", *The Observer:* http://bit.ly/1QFsu9g

Uncle Sam

The national personification of the United States is said to be based on 'fair, reliable and honest' Upstate New Yorker Samuel Wilson, a meat packer who supplied the US army during the War of 1812 with Great Britain. But the famous World War I poster of Uncle Sam – depicting a silver fox with a goatee, swallow-tailed coat and tall hat who's pointing at the viewer and declaring: "I want you for U.S. Army" – was created a hundred years later by someone whose search for the ultimate symbol of America ended as soon as he looked in the mirror.

Based on the UK's "Lord Kitchener Wants You" call to arms, the poster features an older version of its creator, James Montgomery Flagg. It was again used for recruitment during WWII, when President Franklin D. Roosevelt acknowledged the underlying vanity of the design, telling the artist: "I congratulate you on your resourcefulness in saving model hire. Your method suggests Yankee forebears."

Further reading:

"The Most Famous Poster", Library of Congress: http://bit.ly/2fLsTSA

Fourth of July or Second of July?

While the Fourth of July is known as Independence Day, it commemorates the approval of the final version of the Declaration of Independence rather than the formal decision to create the USA, which had, in fact, been taken two days earlier, on 2 July 1776.

Although celebrations to mark the secession of thirteen British colonies in North America have always been held on July Fourth, one of the Founding Fathers of the United States, John Adams, who later became its second President, didn't expect that to be the case at the time, writing to his wife, Abigail, on the day after the vote to sever political ties with Great Britain: "The Second Day of July 1776, will be the most memorable Epocha, in the History of America. I am apt to believe that it will be celebrated, by succeeding Generations, as the great anniversary Festival."

Further reading:

"John Adams to Abigail Adams, 3 July 1776", US National Archives: http://bit.ly/2uhGy6j

CHAPTER EIGHT
"I had a dream"

At 3.07 on Tuesday morning, the President of the United States was still sitting in his high-back leather executive chair in the Oval Office, having watched TV non-stop since returning from Charlottesville a few hours earlier. Just as Protesto couldn't take his eyes off the parrot in the bird cage, Trump was unable to drag himself to bed while all channels either mocked or condemned his plans to obliterate the moon. Finally, he couldn't bear it any longer and had to find out if the print media was as scathing.

"Hello munchkin," he softly said into the receiver, when the Treasury Secretary sleepily answered the phone at his Mediterranean-style mansion in DC's wealthy Massachusetts Avenue Heights neighbourhood.

"Mr President," he replied tiredly. "What time is it?"

"It doesn't matter – the TV channels are being nasty to me."

"Sorry, I didn't mean to be insensitive," Mnuchin said, as he slowly woke up.

"They don't even care that I went to Charlottesville like they wanted me to," Trump said angrily.

"I think that's very, very unfair."

"Me, too. And I want to find out if the newspapers are also being unfair, so can you come to the White House and read them out to me?"

"Why don't you have a look at their websites?" the Treasury Secretary suggested.

"Because I'm an audio-visual learner."

"Pardon?"

"I'm an audio-visual learner, so you have to read them out to me."

"Oh, right," Mnuchin said, embarrassed. "I'll be there in fifteen minutes."

When he arrived at the Oval Office, his boss was still glued to the large television on the wall. Pointing towards it, Trump said: "They keep saying nasty things about me – that I'm a bad President and that my plans don't work. And it's not just the fake media like CNN – it's Fox News, as well."

Sitting down in the visitors' chair, the Treasury Secretary looked at the TV, too. But Trump turned his computer slightly to the left and beckoned him to move his chair around, so they could look at the screen together.

"Tell me what Breitbart have written," the President said.

Visiting the website, Mnuchin was relieved to find that there weren't any bad surprises. Having read the main editorial, he said excitedly: "They say your speech in Charlottesville was amazing and that the turnout was amazing, and they also say that it's amazing to finally have a President who stands up to intelligent and educated people and thinks outside the box when it comes to dealing with North Korea."

"Breitbart is very, very trustworthy," Trump said solemnly. "I trust them very, very much." Nodding towards the computer screen, he asked: "And what about the fake media? What does *The New York Times* say?"

Gulping, Mnuchin went to the newspaper's homepage full of links to disdainful features about the President, who pointed at an opinion piece entitled 'The lunatic reaches for the moon' and said: "Click on that one and read it out to me."

Warily, the Treasury Secretary opened the article. Yet just as he was about to read out the headline, he paused, then said: "This piece is called 'The President reaches for the moon'."

"To be successful you have to think bigly," Trump replied, while his aide vetted the first paragraph. "So, what does it say?"

"It says: On May 25, 1961, John F. Kennedy declared before Congress that 'this nation should commit itself to achieving the goal, before the decade is out, of landing a man on the moon and returning him safely to the Earth'," Mnuchin said truthfully. "With a greater sense of urgency, Donald Trump announced a moon mission of a different kind yesterday, saying he would 'blow up the goddamn thing' to achieve high TV ratings at a time when his own approval ratings are plummeting into the gutter, where he's dragged our country, too," the Treasury Secretary read, yet silently this time.

Instead, he said: "They go on comparing your mission to Kennedy's moon landings, and they mention that you're aiming for high TV ratings."

"Do they say what the ratings were for the moon landings?"

"They don't go into that."

"And do they say that my space programme is better than Kennedy's?"

"They don't use the word 'better', but they don't use the word 'worse' either."

Leaning back in his chair, Trump considered the information for a moment. "Well, overall, that's still better than what I'd expected," he said. "I always thought *The New York Times* is just out to get me, but it sounds like I can actually trust them."

Switching off the TV with his remote control, he yawned, got up and ushered Mnuchin towards the door. As they both left the Oval Office and stepped into the hallway of the West Wing, he added: "I'm going to sleep for a couple of hours – I haven't been to bed yet." Then he headed up the stairs and said: "Good night, my munchkin."

Just over an hour later, at five o'clock in the morning, Trump was snoring in his king-sized, four-poster bed in the presidential residence on the second floor of the White House when he suddenly woke up after an unusually vivid dream that had shown him the solution. He immediately got up, went down to the Oval Office, and addressing his thirty-five million Twitter followers, he wrote: "I will hold a TOP SECRET meeting about North Korea today with the Secretary of Defense and our military leaders. Stay tuned – we'll have BIG NEWS!!!"

Twenty minutes later, Jim Mattis rang the President and said: "Sir, I just read your tweet. I'm afraid I wasn't aware that you'd scheduled a meeting for today."

"Well, it's top secret."

"Sir, I'd like to remind you that General Dunford, General Milley and I all agree that nuclear war against North Korea is not an option," the Secretary of Defense said firmly.

"The meeting has nothing to do with nuclear war – my solution is much smarter than that. Come to the White House at seven and I'll tell you my plan."

About an hour and a half later, the President's three military advisers sat down on the other side of his desk and eyed him uneasily.

"Sir," General Dunford, the Chairman of the Joint Chiefs of Staff, said, "let me be very clear: we cannot risk another Korean War!"

"We've never had a Korean War – you're thinking of Vietnam," Trump replied. "I almost fought there. And by the way, I would have defeated the Vietcong if Osama Obama hadn't stabbed me in the back! Anyway, now that I'm President, I will defeat North Korea's Vietcong instead."

"And how are you planning to do that, Sir?" Mattis asked warily.

Smiling, Trump looked at each of them. "I had a dream," he said.

"I beg your pardon."

"The solution came to me in my sleep. There was a cow on the South Lawn in front of the White House whose ass was covered in gold dust, and it kept shitting gold nuggets – and when I say gold nuggets I mean big gold nuggets, bigger than any of you have ever seen."

Perplexed, the three military advisers looked at each other.

"Sir, could you please clarify what that has to do with North Korea?" Mattis said.

"It gave me an idea that is so tremendous we had to have a top-secret meeting straight away." Leaning forward, he added conspiratorially: "What we'll do is, we'll secretly send fifty thousand troops to North Korea and attack those cocksuckers from within their own country."

Baffled, his three advisers looked at each other again.

"How are we going to get fifty thousand troops secretly into North Korea?" Dunford asked.

"By using fake cows whose asses are covered in gold dust," Trump explained. "We'll have them built with heads and tails that can be remote-controlled, so they look real. Then we'll take them to South Korea and put them in a field near the North Korean border, with lots of gold nuggets at their feet. As soon as Kim's border guards tell him about the cows, he'll want them, believe me. So, we'll offer him five thousand cows as a gift, and we'll tell him to open the border for us so we can deliver them in five thousand trucks. And in each truck, we'll hide ten soldiers under an elevated floor, which we'll cover with gold nuggets, so that it looks like the cows have been shitting all over the place. And bang, suddenly, we'll have fifty thousand troops in North Korea and blow up the Vietcong from within!"

Taken aback, the three advisers turned to each other once more.

"Sir," Mattis said, and cleared his voice. "With all due respect, this plan sounds, er, unfeasible."

"Have you got any better ideas?" he snapped.

"Sir," General Dunford said, "our intelligence suggests that although Kim Jong-un is deluded and therefore dangerous, he is not stupid."

"Screw intelligence! Kim is a stupid son of a bitch – I know he is, I almost met him – and he'll fall for it, believe me."

"I think we're much more likely to get anywhere with him by using traditional diplomatic channels and by applying pressure through economic sanctions," Mattis said.

"I agree," the Chief of Staff of the Army, Mark Milley, replied.

"War with North Korea should be avoided at all cost," Dunford seconded.

"Sorry, am I missing something?" Trump asked, and frowned at them. "Who is the Commander in Chief?" He looked at all three, but none of them dared to say anything. "Dunford?"

"You are, Sir."

"Milley?"

"You are, Sir."

"Mattis?"

"You are, Sir."

"Right, that's what I thought. And unlike the three of you, I'm not going to pussyfoot around North Korea any longer.

And since you're trying to stand in my way, I will relieve all of you of your duties."

"Sir, you can't do that!" Dunford exclaimed.

"Yes, I can," he coldly replied. "I'm the Commander in Chief, remember? And I'll tell you another thing: I will also cancel your government pensions and redirect the money to the taxpayer, so we can use it for the new Trump hotel I'm going to build in New York." Then he pointed at the door and added: "You're fired!"

As the three men reluctantly exited the Oval Office, he turned to his computer, logged on to Twitter and wrote: "Congratulations, Ivanka, on becoming the new Secretary of Defense. Very proud moment for your Dad!"

Afterwards, he phoned Theresa May to tell her that the UK was to pay for Operation Gold Dust, which wasn't announced on social media and also kept secret from its fake, dishonest cousin. A week later, General Brooks, the Commander of the US forces in South Korea, oversaw the successful mission to deposit the quickly assembled replica herd in a field near the border in the dead of night. As the President had predicted, Kim Jong-un desperately wanted those cows, and once a generous offer of gold-crapping cattle had been extended and accepted via backchannels, fifty thousand US troops secretly entered Pyongyang and took over the city and the presidential palace.

To the world's utter surprise, the mission was officially announced two days later, when all of North Korea had been taken and Kim was transferred to Washington to stand trial. He was accompanied by General Brooks, who'd been invited to the White House to witness the completion of what CNN and *The New York Times* grudgingly called "a deserved tribute": the new Trump Monument.

Standing solemnly in front of the huge gold-plated obelisk on the South Lawn – with Conway, Mnuchin, et al., as well as dozens of reporters nearby – the President and the general placed a wreath at the foot of the memorial.

"What's the wreath for?" Brooks whispered, as they bent down. "None of our soldiers died in the assault."

"You always lay a wreath after winning a war," Trump replied. "I did it after Vietnam, too."

"But, Sir, we didn't win the war in Vietnam, and you didn't fight there either," Brooks said. Noticing that the President was scowling at him, he quickly added: "But we defeated the Vietcong in North Korea!"

Instantly, the frown on Trump's face disappeared, and smiling broadly, he said: "Yes, what a tremendous victory, Brooks – the best! It made me realise that I can trust you." Putting his hand on the general's shoulder while Conway and Mnuchin pricked up their ears and watched them closely, he added: "In fact, I trust you more than anybody else."

Gold turds

In the fourth century BC, King Hui of Qin – the great-great-great-grandfather of China's first emperor – was cosying up to King Kaiming XII of Shu in today's Sichuan province, giving him gifts with the ultimate goal of screwing him over and taking his territory. Yet this was easier said than done since the Shu people's mountainous terrain was difficult to access. Luckily for King Hui, however, the Shu were a bit dim, or at least "unenlightened", as historian John Keay puts it, "even by Qin's doubtful standards".

Aware of their gullibility, he allegedly had five stone cows built that, to Shu eyes, looked indistinguishable from the real thing. Yet it was the added twist of gold-painted backsides and the gold 'turds' at the cattle's feet that truly captured their imagination. Having spotted the strategically placed herd on a patch of grass near their base, some royal emissaries reported back to King Kaiming, who instantly knew this was a no-brainer. So, he asked his friend King Hui to give him the supposedly gold-pooing cows as a present. The latter pointed out that it was impossible to transport them across the inaccessible mountains into Shu. Yet he kindly offered to build a road for that purpose, which meant they had a deal.

But the "celestial cattle" failed to perform as expected, so Kaiming soon returned the gift. And he didn't hold a grudge, though he probably did when King Hui used his newly built Stone Cattle Road – traces of which have been discovered, though the story about its origins may be just a legend – to invade Shu and defeat him in 316BC.

Further reading:

China: A History by John Keay

Ancient Sichuan and the Unification of China by Steven F. Sage

About the author

Based in London, David Hutter studied creative writing at university and has worked as a writer and editor for various publications for more than ten years.

Get in touch

Visit his website to find out more about the idea behind this book and his upcoming novels, or to drop him a line: davidhutter.net

Printed in Great Britain
by Amazon